AMERICAN TALL TALES

AMERICAN TALL TALES

by Mary Pope Osborne

Wood engravings by Michael McCurdy

SCHOLASTIC INC.
New York Toronto London Auckland Sydney

ISBN 0-590-46483-3

Text copyright © 1991 by Mary Pope Osborne. Illustrations copyright © 1991 by Michael McCurdy. All rights reserved. Published by Scholastic Inc., 730 Broadway, New York, NY 10003, by arrangement with Alfred A. Knopf, Inc., an imprint of Random House, Inc.

12 11 10 9 8 7 6 5 4 3 2 1   2 3 4 5 6 7/9

Printed in the U.S.A.   37

First Scholastic printing, September 1992

The wood engravings for this book were cut from single blocks of end-grain maple, and the color was added with watercolor to the final print.

CONTENTS

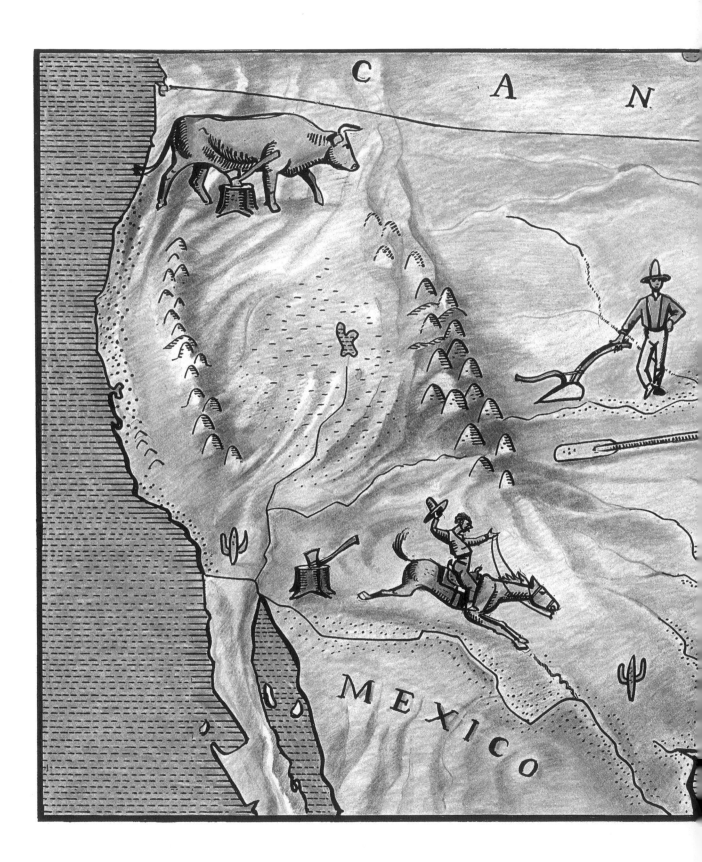

-  — Davy Crockett

Sally Ann Thunder
Ann Whirlwind —

- — Johnny Appleseed

Stormalong —

- — Mose

Febold Feboldson —

- — Pecos Bill

John Henry —

- — Paul Bunyan

INTRODUCTION

TALL TALK, OR EXAGGERATED storytelling, began in the 1800s as a way for Americans to come to terms with the vast and inhospitable lands they'd come to inhabit—thick, dark forests filled with bears and panthers; treeless, arid deserts and plains; towering mountains; and uncharted seacoasts. The heroes and heroines of the tales were like the land itself—gigantic, extravagant, restless, and flamboyant. Their exaggerated feats of courage and endurance helped the backwoodsman face the overwhelming task of developing such a land. "Every time Davy Crockett triumphed over 'man, varmint, and the cogwheels of the universe,'" writes Kenneth S. Lynn, the author of *Mark Twain and Southwestern Humor,* "the ordinary backwoodsman felt an identification with his own efforts to tame his part of the American woods."

The tall-tale characters in this collection were born from various combinations of historical fact, the storytelling of ordinary people, and the imagination of professional writers. Davy Crockett and Johnny Appleseed, for instance, were actual people who lived in the first half of the 1800s. Over a period of time, as their stories were told around campfires, in barrooms, and on steamboats, the true details of their lives were exaggerated and revised until they became folk heroes as well as historical figures.

Other tall-tale characters, such as Pecos Bill and Febold Feboldson, were not actual men of history. Nor were they authentic folk heroes, for their stories were not passed down orally from generation to generation. Instead, these figures were for the most part the literary inventions of professional newspaper and magazine writers. Still, their creators claimed that their yarns were inspired and shaped by the oral tall tales of the 1800s. And as Carolyn S. Brown in her book *The Tall Tale* explains, while there is a folk tall tale and a literary tall tale, we can never "completely disentangle the oral from the written."

A few years ago, while doing research on a biography of Abraham Lincoln, I came across a wonderful passage about Johnny Appleseed written by Carl Sandburg. I found the information so stimulating that I abandoned Lincoln and took my research in a new direction. Johnny led me to Davy Crockett, and Davy led me to Paul Bunyan. Gradually I began to see that a collection of retellings of stories about these characters would paint a rich and colorful map of nineteenth-century America. Not only would the tales reveal a wide range of geographic settings, they would also illustrate the different occupations that contributed to the development of the country. Pioneer settlers, backwoodsmen and -women, sea captains, volunteer firefighters, farmers, cowboys, cowgirls, railroad workers, loggers—all can be found in the American tall tale. I was also attracted by the opportunity the stories provide a writer to combine accurate period detail with larger-than-life characters, to mix reality with wild tall-tale fantasy.

As I combed through old material to select which yarns to retell, I found it disheartening to come across stories that derided African Americans, Native Americans, women, and animals. And considering our environmental problems today, I was less than enthusiastic about the goal of conquering the wilderness at all costs. Therefore, I decided I would attempt to bring out the more vulnerable and compassionate side of the tall-tale characters in my retellings. I sought to revitalize the stories' essential spirit of gargantuan physical courage and absurd humor, de-emphasizing incidents that would seem cruel or insensitive to today's readers. I focused instead on incidents in which the men and women grapple with nature on her terms. I hope that in this collection, as they wrestle with panthers, lasso cyclones, and tramp across the north woods, they also show an abiding respect and affection for the natural world.

Focusing on the humane side of the tall-tale characters not only enabled me to avoid the elements of racial and cultural prejudice in the stories, it also led me to the discovery of a potential tall-tale heroine as well. Surprisingly, it was that backwoods "half-varmint" Davy Crockett, who introduced her to me. "I saw a little woman streaking it along through the woods like all wrath," says the fictional Davy about his wife, Sally Ann Thunder Ann Whirlwind Crockett, in one of the Davy Crockett Almanacks, written between 1835 and 1856.

Davy does not say a great deal more about that intriguing "little woman," but there are quite a few sketches of other extraordinary females in the almanacs. And I thought I owed it to all of them to gather them into one woman and bring her out into the sunlight, where she now stands as tall and proud as her masculine counterparts.

Despite the appearance of Sally Ann and the humanizing of the tall-tale characters, an ineradicable taint of violence still clings to some of these stories. As we prepare to enter the twenty-first century, the survival of this planet is no longer compatible with the nineteenth century's approach of lassoing and taming the environment. But to eliminate that period of our past from our literature is to do children a disservice, I think. I hope these tall-tale stories will provide opportunities for discussion: for contrasting the way it was then with the way it is now—and how it must be in the future; and perhaps for exploring the idea of heroes and heroines in general.

But most of all, I hope that the stories in this collection will provide humor and entertainment, and that both children and adults will have as much fun reading them as I did writing them. While retelling the tall tales, I heard a "distant roarin'." Not only were these exhilarating and rather loony characters laughing and pushing one another around in my imagination, but they introduced others to me as well—"big bears that growled all sorts of low thunder and wolves that howled all sorts o' northeast hurricanes," not to mention all the storytellers and writers that have shared their company in the past. It's been a wild and crowded party, and now we all invite the reader to join us.

I understand the large hearts of heroes,
The courage of present times and all times . . .
　　　　—Walt Whitman

DAVY CROCKETT

NOTES ON THE STORY

THE REAL DAVY CROCKETT was a backwoodsman born in the mountains of Tennessee in 1786. At that time the settlers in the backwoods of Tennessee and Kentucky lived rugged lives devoted to hunting, trapping, clearing the land, and building homesteads. When Davy ran for Congress in 1827, he became famous for satirizing the difficult lives of these frontier men and women. He gained further legendary status after he died at the Alamo in 1836, fighting for Texas in its struggle for independence from Mexico.

Following Davy Crockett's death, a series of small paperbound books were published that contained comically exaggerated tales and woodcuts about his early life. Called the Davy Crockett Almanacks, these books included stories and sayings of the time, and although no one knows who wrote these first American "tall tales," they are still celebrated for their wit and story-telling. Newspapers, songs, plays, television shows, and films have further expanded the Crockett legend, but the following story is derived mostly from these original almanacs.

3

An extraordinary event once occurred in the land of Tennessee. A comet shot out of the sky like a ball of fox fire. But when the comet hit the top of a Tennessee mountain, a baby boy tumbled off and landed upright on his feet. His name was *Davy Crockett.*

That's the same Davy who could carry thunder in his fist and fling lightning from his fingers. That's the same Davy who liked to holler, "I can slide down the slippery ends of rainbows! I'm half horse, half alligator, and a bit of snapping turtle! I can outrun, outlick, and outholler any ring-tailed roarer east of the Mississippi!"

The truth is Davy Crockett did seem to be half varmint—just as every varmint seemed to be half Crockett. Anyone could see that he walked like an ox, ran like a fox, and swam like an eel. And he liked to tell folks, "When I was a baby, my cradle was the shell of a six-hundred-pound turtle! When I was a boy, I ate so much bear meat and drank so much buffalo milk, I could whip my weight in wildcats!" Which was less amazing than you might think, because by the time Davy Crockett was eight years old, he weighed two hundred pounds with his shoes off, his feet clean, and his stomach empty!

Davy Crockett loved to brag about the things he could lick—from wildcats to grizzly bears. Sometimes, though, his bragging got him into big trouble. Take the time he got caught in a thunderstorm in the middle of the forest, carrying nothing but a stick. After hiking some ten miles in the rain, he was so hungry he could have wolfed down a hickory stump, roots and all. He began to search through a black thicket for something good to eat. Just as he parted some trees with his stick, he saw two big eyes staring at him, lit up like a pair of red-hot coals.

Thinking he'd come across a fun fight and a tasty feast combined, Davy neighed like a horse, then hollered like a screech owl. "Hello there! I'm Davy Crockett, and I'm *real* hungry! Which means bad news to any little warm-blooded, four-legged, squinty-eyed, yellow-bellied creature!"

Lightning suddenly lit the woods, and Davy got a good look at his dinner. "By thunder," he breathed. The hair went up on the back of his neck, and his eyes got as big as dogwood blossoms.

Staring back at him was the Big Eater of the Forest—the biggest panther this side of the Mississippi. He was just sitting there with a pile of bones and skulls all around him like pumpkins in a pumpkin patch.

Before Davy could beg the varmint's pardon, the panther spit a sea of froth at him, and his teeth began to grind like a sixty-horsepower sawmill.

"Ohh, I didn't mean what I just said," Davy apologized, backing away slowly.

But the panther shot white fire from his eyes and gave three or four sweeps of his tail as he advanced.

"You think you can forgive me for making a little joke?" Davy begged.

But the panther let out a growl about as loud as five hundred boulders crashing down a mountainside.

"Wanna sing a duet?" Davy asked.

But the panther just growled again and took another step closer.

"Guess I'm going to have to get serious," Davy said, trying to bluff his way out.

The panther stepped forward.

Davy crouched down. "I'm gettin' serious now!" he warned.

But the panther just put his head real low like he was about to leap.

With disaster staring him in the face, Davy suddenly concentrated on grinding his own teeth—until he sounded like a hundred-horsepower sawmill. Then he concentrated on growling his own growl—until he sounded like five thousand boulders tumbling down a mountainside.

As he stepped toward the panther they were both a-grinding and a-growling, until a final growl and a final grate brought the two together. And there in the rainy forest, they began wrestling each other for death or dinner.

Just as the panther was about to make chopped meat out of Davy's head, Davy gave him an upward blow under the jaw. He swung him around like a monkey and throttled him by the neck. And he threw him over one shoulder and twirled him around by his tail.

As Davy was turning the panther into bread dough, the Big Eater *yowled* for mercy.

"Okay, fine, fine," said Davy, panting. "I'm not about to skin such an amazing feller as yourself. But I'm not about to leave you here to collect any more of them bones and skulls, neither. I guess you better come home with me and learn some manners."

So Davy Crockett led the Big Eater of the Forest back to his cabin, and there he taught him all sorts of civilization. Davy taught him how to fold his paws and sing the tenor of a church song and how to rake the leaves with his claws. Best of all, he taught him how to light the hearth fire at night with his burning eyes, then lead Davy to bed in the dark. From then on, you could say that the two were the best of companions.

But Davy's boasting got him into trouble with more than just wild critters. It also nearly ended his political career. It seems that one year he figured the Tennessee Legislature was in sore need of a feller with natural sense instead of book learning. "And that feller is nobody but me!" he bragged as he went about the state, making campaign speeches. "I can sleep under a blanket of snow, outsqueeze a boa constrictor, and outwit the slyest fox in the woods! I'm your man!"

In one of his speeches, Davy got so carried away that he boasted he'd once grinned an old raccoon right out of a tree. "And folks, I can grin *any* dang raccoon out of any dang tree in the whole dang world! If I can't, you can call me a liar and feed me to a bunch of hungry bears in the winter!" he said.

Well, Davy's opponent recognized that this was his big chance to prove once and for all that Davy Crockett was nothing but a blowhard and a boaster. So one moony night in August, the feller got a crowd together, and as they all stood outside Davy's cabin, the varmint hollered, "Crockett, come out here! These folks wanna see your raccoon trick!"

"Sure!" Davy said. "Be glad to show 'em!"

Feeling pretty confident because he believed all his own boasts, Davy led the crowd through the woods, until he spied a raccoon grinning high up in a hickory tree.

"Jimminy crimminy, here I go! Now watch me, folks!" he said, and he set to grinning at the fellow, and he grinned and grinned.

And grinned. But after he'd been grinning like a fool for a spell, that raccoon just kept sitting up in the tree, grinning back down at him, not tumbling down or nothing.

After a while folks began to get restless, and Davy began to get mad. His whole reputation was on the line. He didn't relish being fed to a bunch of bears, neither. He got so mad that he finally stomped home and got an ax. Then he returned to the woods and commenced to cutting down the tree.

Well, when the tree fell and Davy grabbed for the critter, he discovered the grinning raccoon was nothing but an old knothole that looked just like a raccoon!

"But look at this!" Davy said, beaming to the crowd. "The fact is, I done grinned the bark right off of this tree!" He was telling the truth—around the knothole, the tree was perfectly smooth.

"Go figure it," grumbled his opponent as the crowd cheered.

Another tale about Davy's bragging concerned one hot day on the banks of the Mississippi River. As old Davy was straggling along, feeling restless because he hadn't had a fight in ten days, he came across a keelboat being pushed upriver. The fellow pushing it had hair as black as a crow's wing and wore a red flannel shirt. There wasn't a man on the river that wouldn't have recognized Mike Fink, king of the Mississippi Boatmen.

"Hello there!" Davy shouted from the shore. "If you don't watch out, that boat's going to run back down the river! I'm about the only ring-tailed roarer in the world who can tame the Mississippi!"

Mike Fink gave Davy a mean look. "Oh, you don't know beans from buckshot, you old cock-a-doodle-doo," he said.

"Oh! Well, I don't care a johnnycake for you, either!" said Davy. "Come ashore and let me whip you! I've been trying to get a fight going all morning!" Then he flapped his hands near his hips and crowed like a rooster.

Mike Fink, feeling chock-full of fight himself, curved his neck and neighed like a horse.

Davy Crockett thumped his chest and roared like a gorilla.

Mike Fink threw back his head and howled like a wolf.

Davy Crockett arched his back and screamed like a panther.

The two of them kept carrying on—flapping, shaking, thumping, howling, screaming—until they both got too tired to carry on. Then Davy waved his hand. "Farewell, stranger. I'm satisfied now."

"Me too," said Mike. "Feelin' much better myself."

In spite of all his boastin' and braggin' and all his screamin' and fightin', Davy Crockett did do some remarkable things for humankind. Take this story he always liked to tell about himself and the sun:

One day it was so cold, the sunlight froze as fast as it rose. When Davy Crockett saw daybreak was so far behind time, he grew concerned. "I better strike a little fire with my fingers," he said, "light my pipe, and travel a few miles to see what's going on."

Davy brought his knuckles together like two thunderclouds. But the sparks froze before he could even begin to collect them. He had no choice but to start on his way and try to keep himself from freezing. So off he went, hop, skip, and jump, whistling the tune of his favorite song, "Fire in the Mountains." Even then, his hat froze to his head and twenty icicles formed under his nose.

After he'd hopped, skipped, and jumped ten miles up to the peak of Daybreak Hill, Davy Crockett discovered exactly what was going on: The earth had frozen on her axis and couldn't turn around! The reason was, the sun had gotten jammed between two giant cakes of ice.

"Cre-ation!" said Davy. "Something must be done—or human life is over!"

So he took a can of bear grease and poured about a ton of it over the sun's face. Then he kicked the cakes of ice until he wrenched the sun loose. "Move along, Charlie, keep goin'!" he shouted.

In about fifteen seconds, the sun woke up with such a beautiful smile that it made Davy sneeze. Then he lit his pipe with a blaze of sunlight. And as the earth began to move on her axis, he headed on home with a piece of sunrise in his pocket.

SALLY ANN THUNDER ANN WHIRLWIND

NOTES ON THE STORY

THE BACKWOODS WOMEN of Tennessee and Kentucky endured the same hardships as the men as they tried to carve a life out of the wilderness. They helped build cabins and clear land for planting. They hauled water from springs, grew cotton for clothes, and hunted wild animals. Though no early tall tales celebrate an abiding heroine, the Davy Crockett Almanacks do present rugged frontier women in a number of vignettes, such as "Sal Fink, the Mississippi Screamer," "Nance Bowers Taming a Bear," "Katy Goodgrit and the Wolves," and "Sappina Wing and the Crocodile." In these stories the Davy Crockett character tells about comically outrageous women who display amazing boldness and ingenuity.

In the following tale I have chosen to combine these various female characters into a single heroine—and have called her Sally Ann Thunder Ann Whirlwind, the name of Davy's fictional wife, who is briefly mentioned in the Davy Crockett Almanacks.

One early spring day, when the leaves of the white oaks were about as big as a mouse's ear, Davy Crockett set out alone through the forest to do some bear hunting. Suddenly it started raining real hard, and he felt obliged to stop for shelter under a tree. As he shook the rain out of his coonskin cap, he got sleepy, so he laid back into the crotch of the tree, and pretty soon he was snoring.

Davy slept so hard, he didn't wake up until nearly sundown. And when he did, he discovered that somehow or another in all that sleeping his head had gotten stuck in the crotch of the tree, and he couldn't get it out.

Well, Davy roared loud enough to make the tree lose all its little mouse-ear leaves. He twisted and turned and carried on for over an hour, but still that tree wouldn't let go. Just as he was about to give himself up for a goner, he heard a girl say, "What's the matter, stranger?"

Even from his awkward position, he could see that she was extraordinary—tall as a hickory sapling, with arms as big as a keelboat tiller's.

"My head's stuck, sweetie," he said. "And if you help me get it free, I'll give you a pretty little comb."

"Don't call me sweetie," she said. "And don't worry about giving me no pretty little comb, neither. I'll free your old coconut, but just because I want to."

Then this extraordinary girl did something that made Davy's hair stand on end. She reached in a bag and took out a bunch of rattlesnakes. She tied all the wriggly critters together to make a long rope, and as she tied, she kept talking. "I'm not a shy little colt," she said. "And I'm not a little singing nightingale, neither. I can tote a steamboat on my back, outscream a panther, and jump over my own shadow. I can double up crocodiles any day, and I like to wear a hornets' nest for my Sunday bonnet."

As the girl looped the ends of her snake rope to the top of the branch that was trapping Davy, she kept bragging: "I'm a streak of lightning set up edgeways and buttered with quicksilver. I can outgrin, outsnort, outrun, outlift, outsneeze, outsleep, outlie any varmint from Maine to Louisiana. Furthermore, *sweetie,* I can blow out the moonlight and sing a wolf to sleep." Then she pulled on the other end of the snake rope so hard, it seemed as if she might tear the world apart.

The right-hand fork of that big tree bent just about double. Then Davy slid his head out as easy as you please. For a minute he was so dizzy, he couldn't tell up from down. But when he got everything going straight again, he took a good look at that girl. "What's your name, ma'am?"

"Sally Ann Thunder Ann Whirlwind," she said. "But if you mind your manners, you can call me Sally."

From then on Davy Crockett was crazy in love with Sally Ann

Thunder Ann Whirlwind. He asked everyone he knew about her, and everything he heard caused another one of Cupid's arrows to jab him in the gizzard.

"Oh, I know Sally!" the preacher said. "She can dance a rock to pieces and ride a panther bareback!"

"Sally's a good ole friend of mine," the blacksmith said. "Once I seen her crack a walnut with her front teeth."

"Sally's so very special," said the schoolmarm. "She likes to whip across the Salt River, using her apron for a sail and her left leg for a rudder!"

Sally Ann Thunder Ann Whirlwind had a reputation for being funny, too. Her best friend, Lucy, told Davy, "Sally can laugh the bark off a pine tree. She likes to whistle out one side of her mouth while she eats with the other side and grins with the middle!"

According to her friends, Sally could tame about anything in the world, too. They all told Davy about the time she was churning butter and heard something scratching outside. Suddenly the door swung open, and in walked the Great King Bear of the Mud Forest. He'd come to steal one of her smoked hams. Well, before the King Bear could say boo, Sally grabbed a warm dumpling from the pot and stuffed it in his mouth.

The dumpling tasted so good, the King Bear's eyes winked with tears. But then he started to think that Sally might taste pretty good, too. So opening and closing his big old mouth, he backed her right into a corner.

Sally was plenty scared, with her knees a-knocking and her heart a-hammering. But just as the King Bear blew his hot breath in her face, she gathered the courage to say, "Would you like to dance?"

As everybody knows, no bear can resist an invitation to a square dance, so of course the old fellow forgot all about eating Sally and said, "Love to."

Then he bowed real pretty, and the two got to kicking and whooping and swinging each other through the air, as Sally sang:

We are on our way to Baltimore,
With two behind, and two before:
Around, around, around we go,
Where oats, peas, beans, and barley grow!

And while she was singing, Sally tied a string from the bear's ankle to her butter churn, so that all the time the old feller was kicking up his legs and dancing around the room, he was also churning her butter!

And folks loved to tell the story about Sally's encounter with another stinky varmint—only this one was a *human* varmint. It seems that Mike Fink, the riverboat man, decided to scare the toenails off Sally because he was sick and tired of hearing Davy Crockett talk about how great she was.

One evening Mike crept into an old alligator skin and met Sally just as she was taking off to forage in the woods for berries. He spread open his gigantic mouth and made such a howl that he nearly scared himself to death. But Sally paid no more attention to that fool than she would have to a barking puppy dog.

However, when Mike put out his claws to embrace her, her anger rose higher than a Mississippi flood. She threw a flash of eye lightning at him, turning the dark to daylight. Then she pulled out a little toothpick and with a single swing sent the alligator head flying fifty feet! And then to finish him off good, she rolled up her sleeves and knocked Mike Fink clear across the woods and into a muddy swamp.

When the fool came to, Davy Crockett was standing over him. "What in the world happened to you, Mikey?" he asked.

"Well, I—I think I must-a been hit by some kind of wild alligator!" Mike stammered, rubbing his sore head.

Davy smiled, knowing full well it was Sally Ann Thunder Ann Whirlwind just finished giving Mike Fink the only punishment he'd ever known.

That incident caused Cupid's final arrow to jab Davy's gizzard. "Sally's the whole steamboat," he said, meaning she was something great. The next day he put on his best raccoon hat and sallied forth to see her.

When he got within three miles of her cabin, he began to holler her name. His voice was so loud, it whirled through the woods like a hurricane.

Sally looked out and saw the wind a-blowing and the trees a-bending. She heard her name a-thundering through the woods, and her heart began to thump. By now she'd begun to feel that Davy Crockett was the whole steamboat, too. So she put on her best hat—an eagle's nest with a wildcat's tail for a feather—and ran outside.

Just as she stepped out the door, Davy Crockett burst from the woods and jumped onto her porch as fast as a frog. "Sally, darlin'!" he cried. "I think my heart is bustin'! Want to be my wife?"

"Oh, my stars and possum dogs, why not?" she said.

From that day on, Davy Crockett had a hard time acting tough around Sally Ann Thunder Ann Whirlwind. His fightin' and hollerin' had no more effect on her than dropping feathers on a barn floor. At least that's what *she'd* tell you. *He* might say something else.

JOHNNY APPLESEED

NOTES ON THE STORY

IN 1871, W. D. HALEY, a writer for *Harper's New Monthly Magazine*, wrote a biographical essay about a pioneer named John Chapman. Born in Massachusetts in the late 1700s, Chapman moved to the Ohio River Valley as a young man and began planting apple orchards in the wildernesses of Ohio, Indiana, and Illinois. People throughout America heard tales of this barefoot, seed-sowing wanderer. When John Chapman died in 1845, General Sam Houston, standing before Congress, said, "Farewell, dear old eccentric heart. Your labor has been a labor of love, and generations yet unborn will rise up and call you blessed."

Over the years, as legendary details grew out of sketchy historical fact, "Johnny Appleseed," as Chapman came to be called, became an American folk character. Poems, plays, and novels about him proliferated, and monuments were built to honor his memory.

Perhaps Johnny Appleseed represents the immigrants who made amazing contributions to North America by introducing and growing new crops. Certainly it can be said that all of us, including those Johnny Appleseeds of early America, have been inheritors of an even older tradition—the Native Americans' domestication and breeding of wild plants, which first caused our wilderness to flower like a garden.

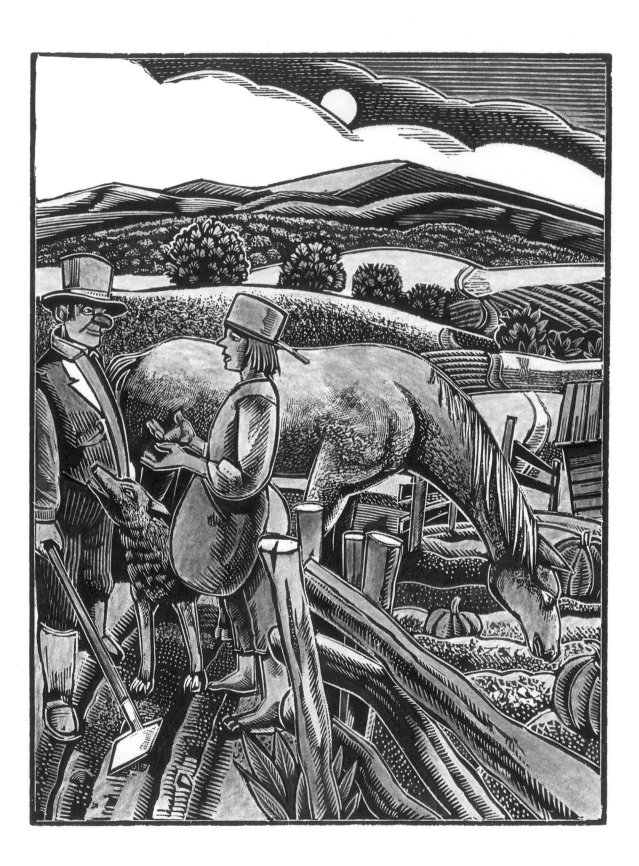

There's a ghost in the Ohio Valley. He moves over the windswept hills and through the apple orchards planted long ago. The farmers in the valley who've heard the ghost singing above the sound of the rustling trees call him by name—*Johnny Apple-seed.*

One morning in the early 1800s, two brothers sat on a misty bank of the Ohio River near Pittsburgh. John and Nathaniel Chapman had recently journeyed from their father's farm in Massachusetts to the hills of western Pennsylvania. Now as they sat watching pioneer families load their chickens, pigs, and farming tools onto rafts and flatboats, John Chapman seemed lost in his thoughts.

Finally John turned to his brother. "I have a new plan," he said.

"What now?" Nathaniel sighed, expecting to hear yet another of his brother's odd ideas.

"I'm going to be a missionary," said John.

Nathaniel laughed. "That's not a *new* plan," he said, for John was always telling Bible stories and reporting his long conversations with angels.

"Not a regular missionary, Nathaniel," said John, his dark eyes shining. "An apple missionary."

"A what?"

"An apple missionary. I'm going to spread apples all over the frontier! Last night I prayed for a sign to tell me how I could help these brave souls traveling to a new life in a new land. I had a dream, and behold"—John stretched out his arm and spread his bony fingers—"I saw apple orchards shining all through the wilderness!"

A rooster crowed in the early-morning air, and Nathaniel Chapman shook his head and smiled. He wished John would settle near him in the Pennsylvania woods. But he knew that nothing he could say would keep his brother from trying to make his apple dream come true.

The next day John Chapman began gathering apple seeds from the sweet-smelling cider mills around Pittsburgh. He dried the seeds in the sun, then packed them into deerskin sacks. When John had enough, Nathaniel helped him load the sacks into two canoes, then lash the canoes together with a rope.

"Good luck!" Nathaniel called, his heart heavy as he watched his strange and remarkable brother row down the Ohio. He hoped John wouldn't be too lonely.

But John Chapman wasn't worried about loneliness. He had a mission. As he paddled his canoe up and down the dark streams that branched out from the Ohio, he called to the settlers fishing and bathing along the banks: "Apple seeds! Take them! Sow them and harvest God's jewels!

"Seeds! Seeds! Apple seeds!" he called, and the settlers rushed

to him and took his seeds and asked him for advice on raising the trees.

But John didn't just give his seeds to others to plant. He soon abandoned his canoes. Then he put his tin coffeepot on his head for a hat, slung one of his deerskin sacks over his shoulder, and headed barefoot into the thick wild woods filled with hickories, willows, and alders. When he came upon a sunny clearing, John dug into the moist brown earth to plant the seeds himself. "There's going to be an apple orchard here someday," he said to the birds and squirrels. "Folks will have all the apples they can eat. So don't go takin' these little seeds, brothers. Wait for the apples."

The woods were filled with bears, wolves, wild hogs, and rattlesnakes, but John never hurt a living thing. He ate nuts and gooseberries, plums and honey. He planted his apple seeds, talked to the animals, and sang in a voice as soft and sweet as the evening breeze.

For days John didn't see a soul in the wilderness. Then one morning he followed a trail that led to a trading post where trappers bartered fur skins and ginseng root for sugar, flour, and coffee.

"Hello, brothers and sisters. I've come to light a candle of understanding!" John said, poking his nose in the doorway. "I've got news fresh from heaven!"

The traders didn't know what to make of this strange barefoot man wearing an old sugar sack for a shirt and a tin pot on his head. They snickered at first. But when John began to talk about apples, his eyes snapping in the lantern light, they stood still and listened. By the time he was ready to leave, they hated to see him go.

"Take these seeds to your families," he said, reaching into his sacks. "They'll bring you fall wine! Winter preserves! Spring blossoms! Summer pies!"

"I'll trade you some cornmeal and coffee for them," the owner of the trading post said to John.

"I won't be needing any food today, brother," John said. "But how about trading for that horse tied up outside?"

"Jim? Why, sure," said the trader, laughing. Everyone could see that the worn-out horse was not long for this world. He could barely stand up in the noon sunshine. John said good-bye to the traders, then led his new friend to a cool stream and poured potfuls of water over his dusty hide. As the bony horse nuzzled John's hand, strange, whimpering cries came from the nearby woods.

John began searching among the trees, following the sounds, until he nearly stumbled over a huge wolf. The wolf's leg was caught in the strong jaws of a steel trap.

"Oh, friend," John gasped. He stooped and pried open the trap. As the animal lay on the ground, John made a splint and bound the wounded leg.

John set up camp by the river and set about nursing the lame wolf and the tired horse back to health. Then the three of them took off together along the old fur traders' trails, crossing the frontier.

As they journeyed through forests and fields, over valleys and along rivers, John Chapman saw a new country growing fast.

He saw the arrival of blacksmiths, potters, weavers, and carpenters.

He saw Yankees from New England and Germans from Pennsylvania traveling in covered wagons and stagecoaches.

He saw the riverboat king, Mike Fink, pushing a keelboat up the Ohio.

He saw steamboats starting to take over the work of the keelboats.

He saw men chopping forests and building canals.

He saw gristmills run by giant waterwheels turning corn into meal.

He saw freight wagons pulled by steam engines running on wooden tracks. Folks called them trains.

He saw mills cutting trees into lumber.

He saw teams of oxen clearing away stumps and roots so farmers could plow the land.

He saw women in sunbonnets gathering pumpkins and corn.

He saw flax drying in the fields and sheep being sheared in the meadows.

He saw buffalo standing in deep grass as flocks of geese flew overhead.

He saw a man named Audubon painting birds on canvas.

He saw a man named Lincoln giving speeches in a field. "Keep it up!" John shouted. "Maybe you'll be president someday!"

For forty years John Chapman traveled the frontier lands between the Ohio River and the northern lakes, carrying his seeds like a bird. He was known in every Indian village and log cabin from the Ohio to Lake Michigan. The Shawnee called him the Appleseed Man and shared their tepees with him. Most of the settlers never knew his last name—they just called him Johnny Appleseed.

One spring night in 1845, as John walked up the road to an Indiana farmhouse, a little girl rushed outside to greet him, crying, "Johnny Appleseed, you've come back!"

"Hi, Rosie. It's good to see you again." And in the cool twilight he hugged her and gave her a bright-blue ribbon and a willow whistle.

"Come inside, Johnny, and join us for dinner," Rosie's mother said.

"Thank you, ma'am, but I think I prefer to eat in the fresh spring air tonight."

As he sat in the twilight, eating his bread and watching the setting sun, he seemed much quieter than usual.

"Johnny, would you like to come in and sleep in front of the fire?" Rosie's father asked when it grew dark.

"No, thank you, William. I'll be just fine in the barn. I like hearing the animals in the dark."

When John laid his tired body down in the soft barn hay, the dogs and chickens and lambs gathered around him. As the moon traveled slowly across the Indiana sky, John listened to the language of the animals, and he answered them in a voice as gentle as the balmy air. "Yes, the wolf should be kind to the lamb," he said, "and the leopard should lie down with the calf. . . . Now quiet, my friends, time to sleep, a little folding of our hands to sleep . . ."

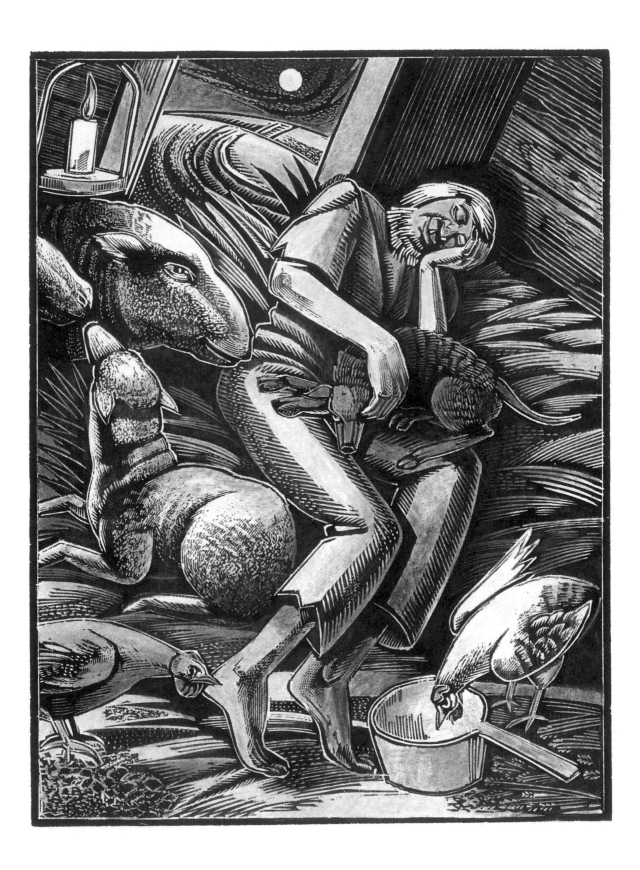

The next morning Rosie's father found Johnny Appleseed lying very still in the hay. The following week the Fort Wayne *Sentinel* had a simple notice:

Died in the neighborhood of this city, on Tuesday last,
Mr. John Chapman,
better known as Johnny Appleseed.

Johnny was gone.

But years later, when Rosie was a very old lady, she told a mysterious story to her great-great granddaughter. It seems that the night Johnny Appleseed died, the birds began to sing joyfully in the midnight dark. Then just before dawn Rosie saw a small, thin man with a tin pot on his head slip from the barn into the forest. The man was followed by an old horse and a lame wolf.

Other folks in the Ohio Valley still say that in the very early morning, before sunrise, if you go to a certain apple orchard at a bend in the river, you'll see smoke rising into the blue morning air. Johnny Appleseed is heating up his coffee over his fire. Soon his spirit will begin moving among the trees, waking the apple blossoms to a new day.

STORMALONG

NOTES ON THE STORY

IN THE 1840s, great wooden ships known as clippers began sailing the high seas. These narrow, swift vessels were considered the fastest ships in the world. They sailed from New England ports to the West Indies, Java, China, and India, carrying furs and bringing back tea and silks. They also sailed around the tip of South America, transporting gold seekers from the east coast of America to California. When the Civil War ended, in 1865, steam-ships—and later, oil-burning ships—took over the work of the clippers. The days of the great wind-driven wooden ships soon came to an end.

Stormalong was first immortalized in "Old Stormalong," a popular sea chantey, or work song, sung by sailors when they weighed anchor or hoisted the sails. In 1930, in his book *Here's Audacity,* Frank Shay collected and retold the old yarns about Stormalong told by sailors from the old wooden ships. And a few years later, a pamphlet published by C. E. Brown brought together more of the Stormalong tales.

The story of Stormalong has since been retold a number of times. The popularity of the tale is due at least in part to the nostalgic, romantic appeal of the tall, graceful clippers and admiration for the skill and physical courage of the sailors who piloted them. Since the fossil fuels that have driven our ships for the last hundred years are in finite supply, perhaps it is just a matter of time before the great wind-driven ships return to the sea.

One day in the early 1800s a tidal wave crashed down on the shores of Cape Cod in New England. After the wave had washed back out to sea, the villagers heard deep, bellowing sounds coming from the beach. When they rushed to find out what was going on, they couldn't believe their eyes. A giant baby three fathoms tall—or eighteen feet!—was crawling across the sand, crying in a voice as loud as a foghorn.

The villagers put the baby in a big wheelbarrow and carried him to town. They took him to the meetinghouse and fed him barrels and barrels of milk. As ten people patted the baby on the back, the minister said, "What will we name him?"

"How about *Alfred Bulltop Stormalong*?" a little boy piped up. "And call him Stormy for short."

The baby smiled at the boy, then let out a giant burp that nearly blew the roof off the meetinghouse.

"Stormy it is!" everyone cried.

As he grew older Stormy was the main attraction of Cape Cod. He didn't care for all the attention, however. It reminded him that he was different from everyone else. After school he always tried to slip away to the sea. He liked to swim out into the deep water and ride the whales and porpoises. Stormy's love for the ocean was so strong that folks used to say he had salt water in his veins.

By the time Stormy was twelve, he was already six fathoms tall—or thirty-six feet! "I guess you're going to have to go out into the world now," his friends said sadly. "The truth is, you've grown too big for this town. You can't fit in the schoolhouse, and you're too tall to work in a store. Maybe you should go to Boston. It's a lot bigger than Cape Cod."

Stormy felt like an outcast as he packed his trunk, hoisted it over his shoulder, and started away. And when he arrived in Boston, he discovered something that made him even sadder. Although the city had more buildings than Cape Cod, they were just as small. Worse than that, his huge size and foghorn voice scared the daylights out of everyone he met.

"A sailor's life is the only one for me," he said, staring longingly at Boston Harbor. "The sea's my best friend. It's with her that I belong." And with his back to Boston, Stormy strode toward the biggest Yankee clipper docked in the harbor, *The Lady of the Sea*.

"Blow me down!" said the captain when Stormy stood before him. "I've never seen a man as big as you before."

"I'm not a man," said Stormy. "I'm twelve years old."

"Blow me down again!" said the captain. "I guess you'll have to be the biggest cabin boy in the world then. Welcome aboard, son."

The sailors were a bit shocked when the captain introduced the thirty-six-foot giant as their new cabin boy. But the day soon came when all the sailors of *The Lady of the Sea* completely accepted Stormy's awesome size. It happened one morning when the clipper was anchored off the coast of South America.

"Hoist the anchor!" the captain shouted after a few hours of deep-sea fishing. But when the crew pulled on the great chain, nothing happened. The sailors heaved and hoed, and still could not move the anchor off the bottom of the ocean.

"Let me take care of it!" Stormy boomed. Then the cabin boy stuck a knife between his teeth, climbed onto the bowsprit, and dived into the sea.

After Stormy disappeared, terrible sounds came from the water. The ship began pitching and tossing on wild, foaming waves. It seemed that all aboard were about to be hurled to a wet grave, when suddenly the sea grew calm again—and Stormy bobbed to the surface!

Hand over hand he climbed the anchor chain, nearly pulling the ship onto her side with his great weight. As soon as he was safely aboard, he yanked up the anchor, and once again *The Lady of the Sea* began to glide through the ocean.

"What happened?" cried the crew.

"Just a little fight with a two-ton octopus," said Stormy.

"Octopus!"

"Aye. He didn't want to let go of our anchor."

"What'd you do to him?" the others cried.

"Wrestled eight slimy tentacles into double knots. It'll take a month o' Sundays for him to untie himself."

From then on Stormy was the most popular sailor on board. Over the next few years his reputation spread too, until all the Yankee clipper crews wanted him to sail with them.

But Stormy still wasn't happy. Partly it was because no ship, not even *The Lady of the Sea,* was big enough for him. She would nearly tip over when he stood close to her rail. All her wood

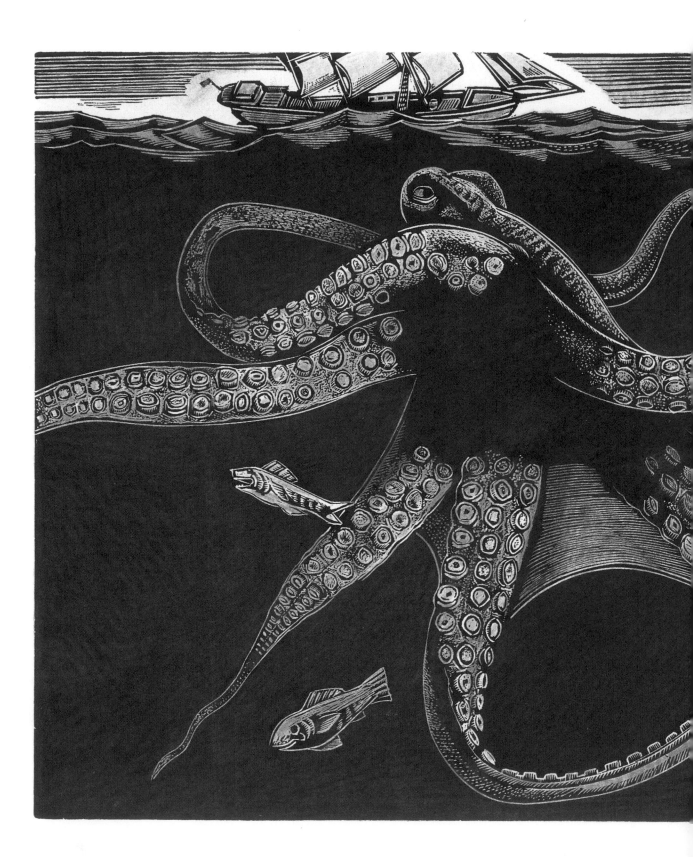

peeled off when he scrubbed her decks. And giant waves rolled over her sides when he sang a sea chantey.

Worst of all, Stormy was still lonely. The clipper's hammocks were so small that at night he had to sleep by himself in a row-boat. As he listened to the other sailors singing and having a good time, he felt as if his best friend, the sea, had betrayed him. Maybe it was time for the giant sailor to move on.

One day, when *The Lady of the Sea* dropped anchor in Boston, Stormy announced to his friends that he'd decided to give up his seafaring life. "I'm going to put an oar over my shoulder and head west," he said. "I hear there's room enough for any kind of folks out there, even ones as big as me."

"Where will you settle down, Stormy?" a sailor asked.

"I'm going to walk till the first person asks me, 'Hey, mister, what's that funny thing you got on your shoulder there?' Then I'll know I'm far enough away from the sea, and I won't ever think about her again."

Stormy walked through the cities of Providence and New York. He walked through the pine barrens of New Jersey and the woods of Pennsylvania. He crossed the Allegheny Mountains and floated on flatboats down the Ohio River.

Pioneers often invited Stormy to share their dinner, but these occasions only made him homesick, for folks always guessed he was a sailor and asked him questions about the sea.

It wasn't until Stormy came to the plains of Kansas that a farmer said, "Hey, mister, what's that funny thing you got on your shoulder?"

"You asked the right question, mate," said Stormy. "I'm going to settle down on this spot and dig me some potatoes!"

And that's just what Stormy did. Soon he became the best farmer around. He planted over five million potatoes and watered his whole crop with the sweat of his brow.

But all the time Stormy was watering, hoeing, picking, and planting, he knew he still had not found a home. He was too big to go square dancing in the dance hall. He was too big to visit other farmhouses, too big for the meetinghouse, too big for the general store.

And he felt a great yearning for the sea. He missed the fishy-smelling breezes and salt spray. Never in the prairies did a giant wave knock him to his knees. Never did a hurricane whirl him across the earth. How could he ever test his true strength and courage?

One day, several years after Stormy's disappearance, the sailors of Boston Harbor saw a giant coming down the wharf, waving his oar above his head. As he approached, they began to whoop with joy. Stormy was back!

But as happy as they were to see him, they were horrified when they discovered how bad he looked. He was all stooped over. His face was like a withered cornstalk, and there were pale bags under his eyes.

After word spread about Stormy's condition, thousands of sailors met to talk about the problem.

"We've got to keep him with us this time," one said.

"There's only one way to do it," said another. "Build a ship that's big enough."

"Aye!" the others agreed. "We can't be having him trail behind us at night in his own rowboat!"

So the New England sailors set about building the biggest clipper ship in the world. Her sails had to be cut and sewn in the Mojave Desert, and after she was built, there was a lumber shortage all over America. It took over forty seamen to manage her pilot's wheel—unless, of course, the captain happened to be Alfred Bulltop Stormalong, who could whirl the ship's wheel with his baby finger!

Stormalong named the clipper *The Courser*. On her maiden voyage, he clutched *The Courser*'s wheel and steered her out of Boston Harbor. As he soared over the billowing waves, his cheeks glowed with sunburn, his hair sparkled with ocean spray, and the salt water began coursing through his veins again.

Soon Stormy and *The Courser* were taking cargoes all over the world—to India, China, and Europe. It took four weeks to get all hands on deck. Teams of white horses carried sailors from stem to stern. The ship's towering masts had to be hinged to let the sun and the moon go by. The tips of the masts were padded so they wouldn't punch holes in the sky. The trip to the crow's nest took so long, the sailors who climbed to the top returned with gray beards. The vessel was so big that once, when she hit an island in the Caribbean Sea, she knocked it clear into the Gulf of Mexico!

But one of *The Courser*'s most memorable escapades took place in the English Channel. When she was trying to sail between Calais and the dark cliffs of Dover, her crew discovered the width of her beam was wider than the passageway.

"It's impossible to wedge her through!" the first mate cried. "We have to turn back!"

"Hurry, before she crashes on the rocks!" said another.

"No, don't turn her back!" bellowed Stormy from the captain's wheel. "Bring all the soap on deck!"

The crew thought Stormy had lost his mind, but they went below and hauled up the three-ton shipment of soap just picked up in Holland.

"Now swab her sides until she's as slippery as an eel," Stormy ordered.

"Aye!" the sailors shouted, and they sang a chantey as they plastered *The Courser*'s sides with white soap.

"Now we'll take her through!" said Stormy. And as the ship's

sails caught the wind, Stormalong eased her between the Dover
cliffs and Calais. Ever since then the white cliffs of Dover have
been as milky white as a whale's belly, and the sea below still
foams with soapsuds.

For years Stormalong was the most famous sea captain in the
world. Sailors in every port told how he ate ostrich eggs for
breakfast, a hundred gallons of whale soup for lunch, and a
warehouseful of shark meat for dinner. They told how after every

meal he'd pick his teeth with an eighteen-foot oar—some said it was the same oar he once carried to Kansas.

But it was also said that sometimes when the crew sang chanteys late at night, their giant captain would stand alone on the deck, gazing out at the sea with a look of unfathomable sorrow in his eyes.

After the Civil War, steamships began to transport cargo over the seas. The days of the great sailing ships came to an end, and the courageous men who steered the beautiful Yankee clippers across the oceans also began to disappear.

No one remembers quite how old Stormalong died. All they recollect is his funeral. It seems that one foggy twilight thousands of sailors attended his burial. They covered him with a hundred yards of the finest Chinese silk, and then fifty sailors carried his huge coffin to a grave near the sea. As they dug into the sand with silver spades and lowered his coffin with a silver cord, they wept tears like rain.

And for years afterward they sang about him:

> *Old Stormy's dead and gone to rest—*
> *To my way, hey, Stormalong!*
> *Of all the sailors he was the best—*
> *Aye, aye, aye, Mister Stormalong!*

Ever since then seamen first class put "A.B.S." after their names. Most people think it means "Able-Bodied Seaman." But the old New England seafaring men know different. They know it stands for the most amazing deep-water sailor who ever lived, Alfred Bulltop Stormalong.

MOSE

NOTES ON THE STORY

In 1848, AMERICA's first urban folk hero was born on the Broadway stage. The play was *A Glance at New York,* by B. A. Baker, and its hero was Mose, the "Bowery B'hoy." Baker based the character Mose on an actual person, Mose Humphreys, a resident of the Bowery and a well-known volunteer firefighter. At that time the old fire machines of New York were hardly more than wagons with hoses. But these "pumpers" were proudly pulled through the streets by the four thousand volunteer "fireboys" of the city.

A Glance at New York was one of the biggest hits of the nineteenth-century American theater. Other plays about Mose followed, and before long, stories about him were published in newspapers and booklets, and his picture began to appear on posters and lithographs. After the Civil War, however, the development of steam fire engines, requiring far less manpower, rendered the old pumpers obsolete. The volunteer firefighters were replaced by a professional force, and the Mose craze came to an end.

Nevertheless, for years afterward tales about Mose continued to spring up, and in 1915 a historian named Herbert Asbury claimed that he collected Mose stories from the old men on the Bowery and included them in his books *The Gangs of New York* and *Ye Olde Fire Laddies.* This tale draws mainly from Asbury's stories and from B. A. Baker's *A Glance at New York.*

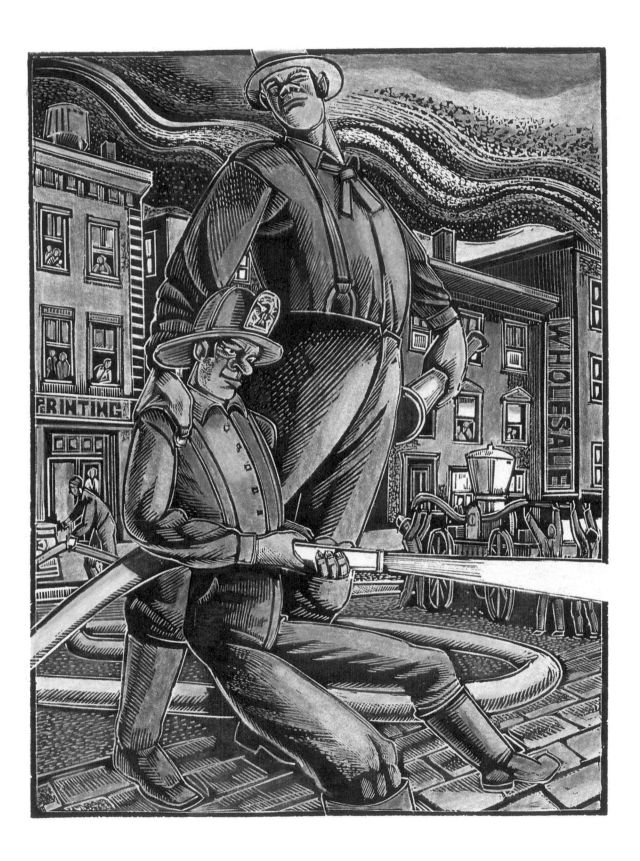

"Afternoon, Mac!" Mose Humphreys tipped his stovepipe hat, revealing his flaming red hair. Puffing a huge cigar, he swaggered toward his special table at the Paradise Soup House on the Bowery. Mose was eight feet tall and had hands as large as Virginia hams. His arms were so long that he could scratch his kneecaps without bending his back.

"Hi, Mose! What'll it be?" shouted Mac, one of the soup house waiters.

Mose sat down in the big chair made especially for him and said, "Bring me a plate of pork and beans, Mac."

But just then cries came from outside—"Fire! Fire! Turn out! Turn out!"—and the fire-alarm bell jangled from the City Hall tower.

A newsboy burst into the soup house, shouting, "Front Street tenement on fire! Spreading fast!"

Mose bounded out of the soup house. As an eerie glow lit up

the evening sky of New York City, he hurried to his fire station. Other volunteer firemen rushed out of workshops, ballrooms, shipyards, and factories, until soon twenty-nine brawny men had joined Mose at the station house.

They all pulled on their bright-red shirts and rainbow suspenders. Then they rolled out their old fire machine, *Lady Washington*. The machine was hardly more than a pump. She had no engine or horses to move her along, so Mose and his men grabbed the old pumper by her two wooden bars and began lugging her through the streets to the fire.

As Mose and the other volunteers clattered over the cobble-stoned streets of old New York City, they ran past the steamboat pier.

They ran past horse liveries and wooden shanties.

They ran past soup houses, pigsties, roosters, and ragmen.

They ran past newsboys crying, "Papers, one cent!"

They ran past oystermen lowering their traps into the Hudson River.

They ran past chimney sweeps, and women shouting, "Apples for sale!" and nurserymaids pushing carriages.

But suddenly the firemen came to a halt. A horse-drawn trolley was stopped in the middle of the road, blocking their path.

"Move! Fire!" Mose cried.

"I can't! She's stuck!" the trolley driver shouted. "One of her wheels is caught between the tracks!"

"I'll take care of it, boys!" Mose shouted to his men. He quickly unhooked the horses from the trolley car. Then he rolled up his sleeves and placed his huge hands under the trolley. Grunting and groaning, Mose lifted the crowded car slowly into the air— until he held it with just one long arm over his head, like a waiter carrying a tray.

As the trolley passengers screamed, Mose staggered across the

street, then slowly set the trolley car down. After he dusted off his hands, he returned to his fire machine. Once again the group of volunteer firemen took off, racing through the streets of old New York toward the black clouds of smoke billowing into the sky.

Hundreds had gathered on Front Street to watch the burning tenement building. As soon as Mose's fire company arrived, he shouted, "Move out of the way!" The crowd quickly parted as the volunteers lugged their pumper to a hydrant.

After Mose hooked up the hose, a team of sixteen men began

pumping the long handles on either side of the machine, to build up pressure to form a jet of water.

But suddenly a woman ran toward the volunteers, screaming, "My baby's on the third floor!"

"Hold the nozzle, boys," Mose said, handing the hose to his men. He grabbed his fire ladder. But when he threw it against the tenement, he discovered it wasn't long enough to reach the third-floor window.

"Bring me a whiskey barrel!" he cried.

When someone brought him the barrel, Mose set the ladder on top of it, then started to climb. The crowd screamed as the ladder swayed left and right.

Mose climbed to a window on the third floor. Then, using his ax, he hacked the wood to make room to wedge his giant body inside. Just as he disappeared into the smoke and flames, the roof of the building began to cave in.

"Nobody can escape now!" someone cried.

Moments later Mose reappeared at the hacked-out window, coughing and covered with soot.

"He's alone!" the mother screamed. "Where's my baby?"

Flames engulfed the tenement as Mose held his stovepipe hat to his chest and started down the ladder. When the ladder caught fire too, Mose leaped into the air, still holding his hat.

Mose landed on the ground, jumped up, and moved quickly out of the way as the tenement collapsed.

The crowd rushed toward him, but Mose pushed them back and shouted, "Where's the baby's mother?"

When the sobbing woman stumbled over, Mose reached into his big hat and pulled out a tiny, crying infant.

"Oh, thank you!" the woman cried as she hugged her child.

"Just doing my duty, ma'am," Mose said.

The volunteers returned *Lady Washington* to the fire station,

and when she was safely put away, Mose resumed his seat across the street at the Paradise Soup House.

"Don't forget about that plate of pork and beans, Mac," he said. "Make it a large piece of pork, and don't stop to count the beans."

Mose Humphreys was famous all over New York City. Boys and girls would follow him everywhere. He could cross the Hudson River with two breaststrokes, and with six he could swim all the way around the island of Manhattan.

Mose's laughter caused the tenement buildings to sway as if in a storm. And when he was angry, his shouting sounded like a trolley car rumbling over the rails. If his old neighborhood gang, the Bowery Boys, got into a scrape with their rivals, the

Dead Rabbits, Mose immediately came to the rescue. Once, when the Dead Rabbits wrecked the Bowery Boys' headquarters, Mose ran after the vandals, hurling huge paving blocks from the sidewalk. He even hurled lampposts before his anger cooled.

But most of all Mose was known as the city's most valiant volunteer fireman. He and his men lugged *Lady Washington* to fires all over the city—in shanties, mansions, theaters, horse stables, soup houses, and butcher shops. He walked through flames as if he were made of bricks, rescuing bankers, bakers, shoemakers, dressmakers, parlormaids, politicians, gamblers, actors, and tiny little babies.

Though Mose was never paid for his work, the city took good care of him. Soup houses fed him barrels of milk and coffee, bushels of oysters and potatoes, and huge amounts of pork and beans. Ragmen gave him their best garments. Bowery shoeshine boys shined his gigantic hobnailed boots for free.

But one day, quite suddenly, Mose Humphreys discovered that his city didn't need him as much as it once had.

He was playing cards and smoking his cigar at the station house when the city alarm bell started going off.

"Fire! Fire! Turn out! Turn out!"

"She's at the docks, boys!" Mose shouted to his men. He could tell the location of the fire by the number of bell strokes.

Mose and the other volunteers pulled on their suspenders and bright-red shirts. Then they grabbed *Lady Washington*'s wooden bars and started hauling the pumper through the streets.

When they arrived at the docks at the end of Houston Street, they found a huge crowd cheering and screaming. Above the crowd a great arc of water was cascading down onto a burning warehouse.

"Get out of our way!" Mose shouted as his men tried to push through the crowd to a fire hydrant.

But the hordes of people didn't pay much attention to Mose and his men. They were too busy cheering the shiny new horse-drawn steam fire engine that was rapidly putting out the fire.

"Look at that!" a newsboy shouted. "It takes only six men to work her!"

As Mose peered over the heads of the crowd, he saw that indeed the boy was right. One firefighter was stoking the steamer's shiny brass chamber with coal, one was tending to her elegant black horses, and the other four were aiming her mighty hose at the roaring flames.

"Out of my way!" Mose shouted.

"Don't worry, Mose, she's under control," an apple seller called to him cheerfully. "Your old pumper's no match for that machine."

Mose was so angry, he began pacing back and forth, huffing and puffing. As he paced, he listened to the newsboys and fruit sellers.

"The mayor says they'll be all over the city soon."

"Yep. He's hiring professional trained firemen to run those fancy machines."

"Say good-bye to the old pumpers."

"Yeah, and the volunteers, too. Hey, look, the steamer's put out the fire!"

"Things are changin' in this city."

As Mose listened to the newsboys, he started pounding his giant fist into the palm of his hand. He began rocking back and forth with rage. Then suddenly he grabbed the wooden handles of *Lady Washington* and began pushing her toward the river.

"Chief, what are you doing?" one of his men cried.

"Wait!" shouted the others. "Wait!"

But there was no stopping Mose as he picked up speed and started running toward the end of the dock. He gave one last

push, sending the old pumper over the edge of the dock.

The crowd heard a huge *splash!* as *Lady Washington* crashed into the Hudson River. Everyone was silent as Mose slowly turned around. He stared at his fellow volunteers with dazed eyes, then staggered away alone.

Mose disappeared from his old haunts after that. Nobody knew for sure what had happened to him. For years folks speculated on his whereabouts. In soup houses, on steamboat piers, in stale barrooms, they asked, "Heard anything about Mose?"

Sometimes folks answered, "Oh, didn't you hear? He went west and made a fortune in the California gold rush."

"Oh, didn't you hear? He's driving a mule team in the Dakota territory."

"He's leading a wagon train across the country."

"He's part of the pony express."

"He's working for President Lincoln."

But one evening, one of the old fire volunteers, playing checkers on a worn bench near the old station house on the Bowery, had this to say: "If you want to know the truth about Mose, pay attention to me. He's among us still. I seen him hanging around lampposts on cold winter nights. I seen him sleeping in burned-out old tenements. I seen him walking along the foggy wharfs.

"You could say Mose is the spirit of old New York. And when all them shiny new machines decide to break down, and when the city fire-alarm bell starts to ring again, watch out. Because by then, you know, that fireman will have grown to be at least twenty feet tall."

FEBOLD FEBOLDSON

NOTES ON THE STORY

THE LAST AMERICAN FRONTIER of the 1800s to be developed was the Great Plains. When thousands of pioneers crossed the plains, headed for the rich soil in Oregon and, later, for the gold fields of California, many complained that the land was without timber or rainfall and plagued with dust storms and grasshoppers. The land was so bleak that, in 1843, Senator George Duffie of South Carolina said, "The whole region beyond the Rocky Mountains, and a vast tract between that chain and the Mississippi, is a desert . . . which no American citizen should be compelled to inhabit unless as punishment for crime." (Of course, generations of Native Americans had lived happy, self-sufficient lives on the Great Plains, in harmony with the land.)

In order to survive, the farmers who chose to settle on the plains had to rethink their ways of doing things—or come up with new ways entirely. One such farmer, Febold Feboldson, was invented by a Nebraska lumber dealer named Wayne Carroll. A series of tales about Febold were published in 1923 in the *Independent,* a newspaper in Gothenburg, Nebraska. Other yarns about Febold by other authors were printed in the Gothenburg *Times* from 1928 to 1933. And in 1937, Paul Beath collected a number of Febold's deeds and published them in the "Nebraska Folklore" pamphlets. Beath's yarns about Febold provided the basic inspiration for this retelling.

After living on the Great Plains by himself for a year, a Swedish farmer named Febold Feboldson grew afraid that he might die of loneliness. As he watched wagon trains bump over the prairies on their way to California, he waved his straw hat and shouted, "Stay here! Live here!"

But Febold always got the same answer: "No, thanky. We're going to look for gold!"

Instead of giving up, the broad-shouldered, sunburned Swede sat down and cupped his jaw in his giant hand and tried to figure out a way to make the gold hunters settle near him on the plains. In three seconds Febold came up with about a hundred great ideas. But the idea that made him do a little dance was this: order a thousand goldfish from Peru.

Febold ordered the goldfish, and when they arrived, he dumped all of them in a lake near his sod shanty—the only lake on the whole prairie. Then the crafty farmer hid in the tall grass and waited for the prairie schooners to roll by.

It wasn't long before a small wagon train clattered over the hard-baked earth near Febold's farm.

"Look, look! Gold!" a pioneer woman shrieked when she saw something glittering in the sunlit lake.

Febold grinned as the pioneers jumped off their wagons and charged across the prairie. From the tall grass he watched the pioneers dipping their pans into the water. They chattered like magpies, and Febold's heart soared with joy. He saw wonderful times ahead, sharing his life with good neighbors.

But as the pioneers panned for gold, the terrible dry weather of the plains began to get to them. It was so hot, they were soon forced to jump into the lake to keep from drying up and blowing away altogether.

"Folks, this is a terrible place to live," said Olaf Swenson, the wagon master. "It's too hot and dry. It never rains. And we haven't found any gold in this lake all day."

"You're right, Olaf. Let's move on to California," said the others. With their tongues hanging out, they all ran back to the wagon train.

As the pioneers climbed aboard their wagons, Febold saw his precious dream of having neighbors start to evaporate. Before anyone could say giddy-yap, he jumped out of the grass and screamed, "*Wait!* Stay here tonight, neighbors, and I promise you some rain."

A tall order, but Febold was desperate. He thought and thought, until he came up with about a hundred great ideas. But the idea that made him do a little dance was this: build a big bonfire beside the lake.

The bonfire Febold built was so big and burned so hot that soon the water in the lake vaporized and formed clouds over the prairie. The clouds were so big and so heavy that when they

rolled into one another, it started to rain. Buckets and buckets of rain!

The problem was, none of the rain hit the ground. Why? Because the air was so hot and so dry that the rain turned to steam before it even touched the land. And what happens when steam and dry land meet? Fog. So much fog covered the plains that the pioneers couldn't see a thing.

"This is awful," said Olaf, groping toward his wife, Anna.

"It sure is. Let's get out of here," said Anna.

But as they stumbled back toward their wagon, Febold shouted, "*Wait!* I'll get rid of the fog." Then he ran into his shanty and came out with a giant pair of clippers.

The pioneers gaped as Febold snipped the fog into long strips. Then they watched him bury the strips in his field. When all the fog was buried, the rain from the clouds crashed to the ground! And everyone shouted with joy.

But then a silly thing happened—a thin piece of the fog seeped out of the ground and wafted through the air. It looked just like a ghost, and when the clouds saw it, they ran away in fright—leaving the day right back where it had begun: unbearably hot and dry.

"We can't live here without rain!" cried Olaf.

"*Wait!*" said Febold. "I'll get more rain. Just give me a minute to think." He cupped his large jaw in his giant hand and thought and thought—until suddenly he came up with a plan.

"Noise!" he announced.

"Noise?" asked Anna.

"Didn't you ever notice it always rains when there's a lot of noise? Fourth of July fireworks? Parades? Battles? Outdoor dances?"

"Well . . ." said Olaf.

"And nothing makes more noise than *frogs*!" Febold said.

The pioneers rolled their eyes at each other, but before they could say anything, Febold ran out into the fields, gathering all the frogs that lived on his farm. Thousands of them! Frogs of all sizes and dispositions!

His plan was not as simple as it looked, though, for he soon discovered that frogs make noise only when they're good and wet. So he grabbed one cheerful-looking frog and whispered in its tiny ear, "It's raining, it's raining, it's raining."

Febold kept this up until he had completely hypnotized the frog. And when it started to croak, the others began to croak too, and soon every single frog was singing its heart out—and the rains came!

As the rains fell, Olaf, Anna, and the others jumped for joy

and cried, "Yes! We'll stay on the plains and build our farms! Miracles happen in this land!"

But disaster was just around the corner. The next day the pioneers discovered that they couldn't get their fence posts in the ground because the soil was still hard.

"If we can't fence in our properties, how in the world can we tend to our horses, cows, sheep, oxen, dogs, chickens, and children?" asked Olaf. "We can't stay in this terrible place."

Oh, for goodness' sakes, thought Febold. But he just smiled and said, "*Wait.* And I'll teach you an old prairie trick."

He gathered all the pioneers together for a lesson. "This is how you make and keep postholes on the Great Plains," he said.

"One: Bore a bunch of holes in the hard ground. Two: Let the holes freeze all winter. Three: In the spring, before the ground thaws, dig up the holes. Four: When the frozen holes come out of the ground, slap coats of varnish on them. Five: Slip the varnished holes back into the ground. Six: Insert fence posts."

Well, you might say that this was the beginning of a true change of heart for the pioneers. They were so intrigued with Febold's posthole procedure, they were willing to wait for winter to come to try it out. Before they knew it, Febold was teaching them how to make sod shanties with bricks of matted prairie turf, how to grow corn and wheat, how to plow the barren land, and how to fight grasshoppers, tornadoes, dust storms, and prairie fires.

Olaf and Anna grew quite content with their new life. As they walked through the tall, whispering grass in the twilight, they watched the goldfish slapping the dark waters under the moon. They listened to the frog choruses practicing their rain songs. And they smiled at Febold Feboldson as he waved from his shanty and said, "Evening, neighbors."

PECOS BILL

NOTES ON THE STORY

YARNS ABOUT PECOS BILL, "the greatest cowpuncher ever known on either side of the Rockies, from Texas through Montana and on into Canada," first appeared in a 1923 *Century Magazine*. The author of the piece, Edward O'Reilly, wrote the "saga" of Pecos Bill by combining a number of western folklore episodes with the boastful, comic tall-tale language of heroes such as Davy Crockett and Paul Bunyan.

After O'Reilly invented the character of Pecos Bill, many others revised and expanded upon the yarns in dozens of books, articles, poems, recordings, and plays. Pecos Bill seemed to capture the spirit of an earlier America—wild, untamed, and unsocialized. He even added an occasional note of his own brand of recklessness to stories about other tall-tale characters as well. In an original Febold Feboldson story, Febold and Pecos Bill have a shoot-out. And in a Paul Bunyan anthology, Pecos Bill teaches Paul how to ride a streak of lightning. This tale about Pecos Bill was derived from the O'Reilly saga as well as a number of other retellings.

Ask any coyote near the Pecos River in western Texas who was the best cowboy who ever lived, and he'll throw back his head and howl, "Ah-hooo!" If you didn't know already, that's coyote language for *Pecos Bill*.

When Pecos Bill was a little baby, he was as tough as a pine knot. He teethed on horseshoes instead of teething rings and played with grizzly bears instead of teddy bears. He could have grown up just fine in the untamed land of eastern Texas. But one day his pappy ran in from the fields, hollering, "Pack up, Ma! Neighbors movin' in fifty miles away! It's gettin' too crowded!"

Before sundown Bill's folks loaded their fifteen kids and all their belongings into their covered wagon and started west.

As they clattered across the desolate land of western Texas, the crushing heat nearly drove them all crazy. Baby Bill got so hot and cross that he began to wallop his big brothers. Pretty soon all fifteen kids were going at one another tooth and nail.

Before they turned each other into catfish bait, Bill fell out of the wagon and landed *kerplop* on the sun-scorched desert.

The others were so busy fighting that they didn't even notice the baby was missing until it was too late to do anything about it.

Well, tough little Bill just sat there in the dirt, watching his family rattle off in a cloud of dust, until an old coyote walked over and sniffed him.

"Goo-goo!" Bill said.

Now it's an amazing coincidence, but "Goo-goo" happens to mean something similar to "Glad to meet you" in coyote language. Naturally the old coyote figured he'd come across one of his own kind. He gave Bill a big lick and picked him up by the scruff of the neck and carried him home to his den.

Bill soon discovered the coyote's kinfolk were about the wildest, roughest bunch you could imagine. Before he knew it, he was roaming the prairies with the pack. He howled at the moon, sniffed the brush, and chased lizards across the sand. He was having such a good time, scuttling about naked and dirty on all fours, that he completely forgot what it was like to be a human.

Pecos Bill's coyote days came to an end about seventeen years later. One evening as he was sniffing the sagebrush, a cowpoke came loping by on a big horse. "Hey, you!" he shouted. "What in the world are you?"

Bill sat on his haunches and stared at the feller.

"What *are* you?" asked the cowpoke again.

"Varmint," said Bill hoarsely, for he hadn't used his human voice in seventeen years.

"No, you ain't!"

"Yeah, I am. I got fleas, don't I?"

"Well, that don't mean nothing. A lot of Texans got fleas. The thing varmints got that you ain't got is a tail."

"Oh, yes, I do have a tail," said Pecos Bill.

"Lemme see it then," said the cowpoke.

Bill turned around to look at his rear end, and for the first time in his life he realized he didn't have a tail.

"Dang," he said. "But if I'm not a varmint, what am I?"

"You're a cowboy! So start acting like one!"

Bill just growled at the feller like any coyote worth his salt would. But deep down in his heart of hearts he knew the cowpoke was right. For the last seventeen years he'd had a sneaking suspicion that he was different from that pack of coyotes. For one thing, none of them seemed to smell quite as bad as he did.

So with a heavy heart he said good-bye to his four-legged friends and took off with the cowpoke for the nearest ranch.

Acting like a human wasn't all that easy for Pecos Bill. Even though he soon started dressing right, he never bothered to shave or comb his hair. He'd just throw some water on his face in the morning and go around the rest of the day looking like a wet dog. Ignorant cowpokes claimed Bill wasn't too smart. Some of the meaner ones liked to joke that he wore a ten-dollar hat on a five-cent head.

The truth was Pecos Bill would soon prove to be one of the greatest cowboys who ever lived. He just needed to find the kind of folks who'd appreciate him. One night when he was licking his dinner plate, his ears perked up. A couple of ranch hands were going on about a gang of wild cowboys.

"Yep. Those fellas are more animal than human," one ranch hand was saying.

"Yep. Them's the toughest bunch I ever come across. Heck, they're so tough, they can kick fire out of flint rock with their bare toes!"

"Yep. 'N' they like to bite nails in half for fun!"

"Who are these fellers?" asked Bill.

"The Hell's Gate Gang," said the ranch hand. "The mangiest, meanest, most low-down bunch of low-life varmints that ever grew hair."

"Sounds like my kind of folks," said Bill, and before anyone could holler whoa, he jumped on his horse and took off for Hell's Gate Canyon.

Bill hadn't gone far when disaster struck. His horse stepped in a hole and broke its ankle.

"Dang!" said Bill as he stumbled up from the spill. He draped the lame critter around his neck and hurried on.

After he'd walked about a hundred more miles, Bill heard some

78

mean rattling. Then a fifty-foot rattlesnake reared up its ugly head and stuck out its long, forked tongue, ready to fight.

"Knock it off, you scaly-hided fool. I'm in a hurry," Bill said.

The snake didn't give a spit for Bill's plans. He just rattled on.

Before the cussed varmint could strike, Bill had no choice but to knock him cross-eyed. "Hey, feller," he said, holding up the dazed snake. "I like your spunk. Come go with us." Then he wrapped the rattler around his arm and continued on his way.

After Bill had hiked another hundred miles with his horse around his neck and his snake around his arm, he heard a terrible growl. A huge mountain lion was crouching on a cliff, getting ready to leap on top of him.

"Don't jump, you mangy bobtailed fleabag!" Bill said.

Well, call any mountain lion a mangy bobtailed fleabag, and he'll jump on your back for sure. After this one leaped onto Bill, so much fur began to fly that it darkened the sky. Bill wrestled that mountain lion into a headlock, then squeezed him so tight that the big cat had to cry uncle.

When the embarrassed old critter started to slink off, Bill felt sorry for him. "Aw, c'mon, you big silly," he said. "You're more like me than most humans I meet."

He saddled up the cat, jumped on his back, and the four of them headed for the canyon, with the mountain lion screeching, the horse neighing, the rattler rattling, and Pecos Bill hollering a wild war whoop.

When the Hell's Gate Gang heard those noises coming from the prairie, they nearly fainted. They dropped their dinner plates, and their faces turned as white as bleached desert bones. Their knees knocked and their six-guns shook.

"Hey, there!" Bill said as he sidled up to their campfire, grinning. "Who's the boss around here?"

A nine-foot feller with ten pistols at his sides stepped forward and in a shaky voice said, "Stranger, I was. But from now on, it'll be you."

"Well, thanky, pardner," said Bill. "Get on with your dinner, boys. Don't let me interrupt."

Once Bill settled down with the Hell's Gate Gang, his true genius revealed itself. With his gang's help, he put together the biggest ranch in the southwest. He used New Mexico as a corral and Arizona as a pasture. He invented tarantulas and scorpions as practical jokes. He also invented roping. Some say his rope was exactly as long as the equator; others argue it was two feet shorter.

Things were going fine for Bill until Texas began to suffer the worst drought in its history. It was so dry that all the rivers turned as powdery as biscuit flour. The parched grass was catching fire everywhere. For a while Bill and his gang managed to lasso water from the Rio Grande. When that river dried up, they lassoed water from the Gulf of Mexico.

No matter what he did, though, Bill couldn't get enough water to stay ahead of the drought. All his horses and cows were starting to dry up and blow away like balls of tumbleweed. It was horrible.

Just when the end seemed near, the sky turned a deep shade of purple. From the distant mountains came a terrible roar. The cattle began to stampede, and a huge black funnel of a cyclone appeared, heading straight for Bill's ranch.

The rest of the Hell's Gate Gang shouted, "Help!" and ran.

But Pecos Bill wasn't scared in the least. "Yahoo!" he hollered, and he swung his lariat and lassoed that cyclone around its neck.

Bill held on tight as he got sucked up into the middle of the swirling cloud. He grabbed the cyclone by the ears and pulled himself onto her back. Then he let out a whoop and headed that twister across Texas.

The mighty cyclone bucked, arched, and screamed like a wild bronco. But Pecos Bill just held on with his legs and used his strong hands to wring the rain out of her wind. He wrung out rain that flooded Texas, New Mexico, and Arizona, until finally he slid off the shriveled-up funnel and fell into California. The earth sank about two hundred feet below sea level in the spot where Bill landed, creating the area known today as Death Valley.

"There. That little waterin' should hold things for a while," he said, brushing himself off.

After his cyclone ride, no horse was too wild for Pecos Bill. He soon found a young colt that was as tough as a tiger and as crazy as a streak of lightning. He named the colt Widow Maker and raised him on barbed wire and dynamite. Whenever the two rode together, they back-flipped and somersaulted all over Texas, loving every minute of it.

One day when Bill and Widow Maker were bouncing around the Pecos River, they came across an awesome sight: a wild-looking, red-haired woman riding on the back of the biggest cat-fish Bill had ever seen. The woman looked like she was having a ball, screeching, "Ride 'em, cowgirl!" as the catfish whipped her around in the air.

"What's your name?" Bill shouted.

"Slue-foot Sue! What's it to you?" she said. Then she war-whooped away over the windy water.

Thereafter all Pecos Bill could think of was Slue-foot Sue. He spent more and more time away from the Hell's Gate Gang as he wandered the barren cattle-lands, looking for her. When he fi-

nally found her lonely little cabin, he was so love-struck he reverted to some of his old coyote ways. He sat on his haunches in the moonlight and began a-howling and ah-hooing.

Well, the good news was that Sue had a bit of coyote in her too, so she completely understood Bill's language. She stuck her head out her window and ah-hooed back to him that she loved him, too. Consequently Bill and Sue decided to get married.

On the day of the wedding Sue wore a beautiful white dress with a steel-spring bustle, and Bill appeared in an elegant buckskin suit.

But after a lovely ceremony, a terrible catastrophe occurred. Slue-foot Sue got it into her head that she just had to have a ride on Bill's wild bronco, Widow Maker.

"You can't do that, honey," Bill said. "He won't let any human toss a leg over him but me."

"Don't worry," said Sue. "You know I can ride anything on four legs, not to mention what flies or swims."

Bill tried his best to talk Sue out of it, but she wouldn't listen. She was dying to buck on the back of that bronco. Wearing her white wedding dress with the bustle, she jumped on Widow Maker and kicked him with her spurs.

Well, that bronco didn't need any thorns in his side to start bucking to beat the band. He bounded up in the air with such amazing force that suddenly Sue was flying high into the Texas sky. She flew over plains and mesas, over canyons, deserts, and prairies. She flew so high that she looped over the new moon and fell back to earth.

But when Sue landed on her steel-spring bustle, she rebounded right back into the heavens! As she bounced back and forth between heaven and earth, Bill whirled his lariat above his head, then lassoed her. But instead of bringing Sue back down to earth, he got yanked into the night sky alongside her!

Together Pecos Bill and Slue-foot Sue bounced off the earth and went flying to the moon. And at that point Bill must have gotten some sort of foothold in a moon crater—because neither he nor Sue returned to earth. Not ever.

Folks figure those two must have dug their boot heels into some moon cheese and raised a pack of wild coyotes just like themselves. Texans'll tell you that every time you hear thunder rolling over the desolate land near the Pecos River, it's just Bill's family having a good laugh upstairs. When you hear a strange ah-hooing in the dark night, don't be fooled—that's the sound of Bill howling *on* the moon instead of *at* it. And when lights flash across the midnight sky, you can bet it's Bill and Sue riding the backs of some white-hot shooting stars.

JOHN HENRY

NOTES ON THE STORY

AFTER THE CIVIL WAR, the Chesapeake & Ohio Railroad Company laid hundreds of miles of railroad track through West Virginia. These new railroad routes opened up timber and coal lands and created new towns. When the tracks reached the Alleghenies, the railroad company hired more than a thousand laborers to build tunnels through the mountains. The tunnels were created by blasting through the mountain shale. This work was done by "steel drivers," men who drilled steel spikes into the solid rock. Once the holes were drilled, they were packed with dynamite. Since the early West Virginia tunnels had no safety regulations, these tunnel workers were exposed to an early death from the dynamite explosions, falling rock, and lethal dust created by the blasts.

Starting in the 1870s, a black steel driver named John Henry became the subject of many of the work songs sung by railroad-tunnel gangs. Like most work songs, the John Henry songs consisted of a few short lines repeated several times with pauses in between for the stroke of a pick or hammer. Historians disagree about whether John Henry was based on a real man or not. Some believe that he can be traced to John Hardy, a true-life subject of popular ballads who was also a superior steel driver; others believe that a man named John Henry actually worked on the Big Bend tunnel in the Alleghenies.

Whether John Henry was real or mythical, he was a strong, enduring character to many southern black laborers. Later, when songs about him were recorded and played on the radio, he became known to the general public as well.

The night John Henry was born the sky was as black as coal, thunder rolled through the heavens, and the earth trembled.

"This boy is special," the preacher said as folks gathered in the cabin by the river to see the new baby.

In the dim lantern light, John Henry was the most powerful-looking baby folks had ever seen. His arms were as thick as stovepipes. He had great broad shoulders and strong muscles. And as folks stared at him, he opened his eyes and smiled a smile that lit up the southern night.

When John Henry raised his arm, folks gasped and brought their hands to their faces, for they saw that the mighty baby had been born with a hammer in his hand. Then they all began to laugh and felt happier than they had in a long, long time.

John Henry grew up fast in a world that didn't let children stay children for long. Before he was six, he was carrying stones for the railroad gangs that were building tracks through the land of West Virginia.

By the time he was ten, he was hammering steel from dawn till dark. No train whistle in America sang as loud as John Henry's mighty hammer. It rang like silver and shone like gold. It flashed up through the air, making a wide arc more than nineteen feet, then crashed down, driving a steel spike six inches into solid rock.

By the time he was a young man, John Henry was the best steel driver in the whole country. He could hammer for hours without missing a beat, so fast that his hammer moved like lightning. He had to keep a pail of water nearby to cool it down, and he wore out two handles a day. All the railroad bosses wanted John Henry to work for them. When the Chesapeake and Ohio started making a tunnel in the Allegheny Mountains, they asked him to lead their force of steel-driving men.

Soon John Henry was whistling and singing in the early summer light as he walked to work in the mountain tunnel. Beside him was his wife, Lucy, with eyes as bright as stars and hair as wavy as the sea. Lucy was a steel driver herself. At noontime she drove the spikes while John Henry sat with their little boy, Johnny, in the sunny mountain grass and ate his lunch of ham hocks and biscuits with molasses.

Lifting Johnny high into the air, John Henry shouted, "Someday you're going to be a steel-driving man like your daddy!"

July of that summer was the hottest month on record in West Virginia. Working in the terrible heat, many of the steel drivers collapsed by noon. But John Henry tried to protect their jobs by picking up their hammers and doing their work too. One week he did his own work and the work of four others as well. He hammered day and night, barely stopping for meals.

When the men tried to thank John Henry, he just smiled and

said, "A man ain't nothing but a man. He's just got to do his best."

August was hotter than July. One day as the men labored in the white light of the afternoon sun, a city salesman drove up to the work site. "Come see, everybody!" he shouted. "Lookee here at this incredible invention! A steam drill that can drill holes faster than a dozen men working together!"

"Aw, I don't know about that," said the railroad boss, rubbing his grizzly jaw. "I got the best steel driver in the country. His name is John Henry, and he can beat *two* dozen men working together."

"That's impossible," the salesman said. "But if you can prove your hand driller is faster than my steam driller, I'll give you this machine for free."

The boss called to John Henry, "This fellow doubts which of you can drill faster. How about a big contest?"

As John Henry stared at the steam drill, he saw a picture of the future. He saw machines taking over the jobs of the country's finest workers. He saw himself and his friends out of work and begging beside the road. He saw men robbed of their dignity and robbed of their families.

"I'd rather die with my hammer in my hand than let that steam drill run me down," he yelled back. And his boss and friends all cheered.

"That contest will be the death of you, John Henry," Lucy said later. "You got a wife and a child, and if anything happens to you, we won't ever smile again."

John Henry just lifted Johnny into the air and said, "Honey, a man ain't nothing but a man. But a man's always got to do his best. And tomorrow I'm going to take my hammer and drive that steel faster than any machine!"

Lucy put on her best blue dress, and folks came from all over

Ohio, Virginia, and Kentucky. They came from the countryside, and they came from the cities.

At half past six in the morning, John Henry and the salesman with the steam-powered drill stood side by side. Early as it was, the sun was burning hot. There was no breeze. Sweat poured down people's faces like water down a hill.

As the onlookers gathered around the contestants, Little Bill, the worker who loved John Henry the best, said, "There ain't a steam drill anywheres that can beat that man!"

But the city folks, who had staked their hopes on the future of machines, said, "He won't beat that drill unless the rocks in the mountain turn to gold!"

"No, sirree!" said Jimmy, John Henry's oldest friend. "Before that drill wins, he'll make the mountain fall!"

Bang!—the race was on! As the steam-drill salesman turned on the steam, John Henry kissed the smooth handle of his hammer.

At first the steam drill drove the steel twice as fast as John Henry did. But then he grabbed another hammer and started working with a hammer in each hand. He went faster and faster, striking blow after blow as he tunneled into the mountain.

"That man's a mighty man," a city man shouted, "but he'll weaken when the hardest rock is found."

"Not John Henry! Just listen to that steel ring!" Little Bill said.

"I believe these mountains are caving in!" said the city man.

"No, they're not. That's his hammers you hear in the wind," Jimmy cried.

Inside the dark tunnel, where the yellow dust and heat were so thick that most men would have smothered, John Henry hammered faster and faster. As clouds of stone dust billowed from the mouth of the tunnel, the crowd shouted and screamed. John Henry's hammers sounded like ten thousand hammers.

Lucy, Little Bill, and Jimmy cheered when the steam drill was dragged out of the tunnel. Sputtering and spewing, it had broken down.

"Come back now, John Henry!" Lucy shouted.

But John Henry kept hammering, hammering faster than any man had ever hammered before, hammering against all the machines of the future. As his hammer glowed white-hot, he tunneled deeper into the darkness, driving the steel so hard that the

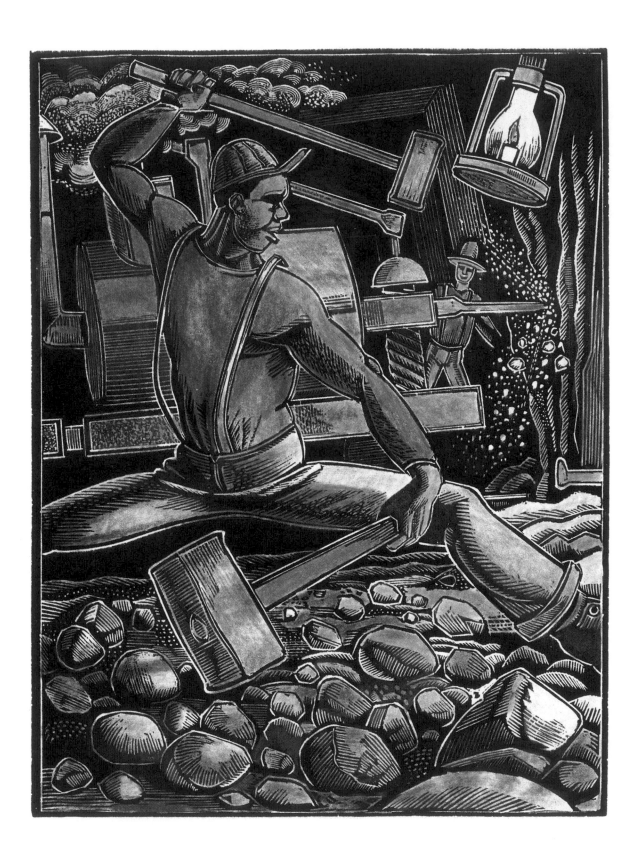

mighty ribs of his body began to crack, and his insides broke in two, and his great heart burst.

When John Henry fell, it sounded like an earthquake.

There was a terrible silence inside the mountain. Lucy stood still as stone, for she knew what had happened.

When Jimmy and Little Bill brought him out of the tunnel, John Henry's blood ran red over the ground. But his hands still clutched one of his mighty hammers. "I've beat them," he gasped. "Now I'm dying."

"Don't go, John Henry!" Lucy begged.

"Bring me a cool drink of water, honey," he said. Then he took his last breath.

Lucy fell down on her knees and sobbed. "Lord, this was a good man," she said.

They carried John Henry down from the mountain. They carried him to the river and buried him in the sand near the cabin where he was born.

Folks stood in the rain and flagged the westbound train headed for John Henry's grave. And word spread quickly across the land: "John Henry's never coming back."

Soon the steam drill and other new machines took over the work of the steel-driving men. Little Bill, Jimmy, and others like them left their families and wandered north and west, looking for work. As they walked the hot, dusty roads, they took the only jobs they could find. They picked cotton and dug ditches. But often while they worked, they sang about John Henry:

John Henry told his friends,
"A man ain't nothing but a man.
Before I'll be beat by that big steam drill,
I'll die with my hammer in my hand,
I'll die with my hammer in my hand."

PAUL BUNYAN

NOTES ON THE STORY

BETWEEN 1870 AND 1900, billions of trees crashed to the ground in New England, the Pacific Northwest, and the woods near the Great Lakes. Sadly, the lumber industry was not concerned then with the conservation of forestland, as it is today. The old-time loggers who claimed to "let daylight into the swamp" had little entertainment at night other than the tales and anecdotes told around the campfires and potbellied stoves. Popular opinion holds that Paul Bunyan was the folk hero of many of the lumberjack tales, though this has been disputed by some old-time lumbermen.

The general public first heard about Paul Bunyan in 1910, when the mythical giant was mentioned in a Detroit newspaper story by James MacGillivray. In 1916, a scholarly paper by K. Bernice Stewart and Professor Homer A. Watt included a collection of Paul Bunyan tales taken directly from loggers of the northern lakes and the Pacific Northwest. Also in 1916, a lumberman named W. B. Laughead wrote a pamphlet for the Red River Lumber Company of Minneapolis. Inserted within advertising copy for the company was a collection of Paul Bunyan stories. Babe the Blue Ox was christened in this pamphlet.

Laughead's Bunyan yarns did not catch on until he rewrote them for a wider audience in the 1920s. At that time Paul Bunyan became very popular, and for the next two decades tall tales about him were frequently published in pamphlets, magazines, and books. This retelling gathers together elements from Laughead's pamphlet as well as from at least a dozen other popularizations of the Paul Bunyan stories.

It seems an amazing baby was once born in the state of Maine. When he was only two weeks old, he weighed more than a hundred pounds, and for breakfast every morning he ate five dozen eggs, ten sacks of potatoes, and a half barrel of mush made from a whole sack of cornmeal. But the baby's strangest feature was his big curly black beard. It was so big and bushy that every morning his poor mother had to comb it with a pine tree.

Except for that beard, the big baby wasn't much trouble to anybody until he was about nine months old. That was when he first started to crawl, and since he weighed over five hundred pounds, he caused an earthquake that shook the whole town.

When the neighbors complained, the baby's parents tried putting him in a giant floating cradle off the coast of Maine. But soon a delegation of citizens went to the baby's parents and said, "We're sorry, folks, but you have to take your son somewhere else. Every time he rolls over in his cradle, huge waves drown all the villages along the coast."

So his parents hauled the giant toddler to a cave in the Maine woods far away from civilization and said good-bye. "We'll think of you often, honey," his mother said, weeping. "But you can't come back home—you're just too big."

"Here, son," his father said. "I'm giving you my ax, my knife, my fishing pole, and some flint rocks. Good-bye and good luck."

After his parents left, the poor bearded baby cried for thirty days and thirty nights. He was so lonely, he cried a whole river of tears. He might have cried himself to death if one day he hadn't heard *flop, flop, flop*.

When the baby looked around, he saw fish jumping in his river of tears. He reached for his father's fishing pole, and soon

he was catching trout. He used his father's knife to clean and scale what he had caught and his father's ax to cut wood for a fire. He started the fire with his flint rocks and cooked his catch over the flames. Then he ate a big fish dinner and smiled for the first time in a month.

That's the story of how Paul Bunyan came to take care of himself in the Maine woods. And even though he lived alone for the next twenty years, he got along quite well. He hunted and fished. He cut down trees and made fires. He battled winter storms, spring floods, summer flies, and autumn gales.

Nothing, however, prepared Paul Bunyan for the wild weather that occurred on the morning of his twenty-first birthday. It was a cold December day, and when Paul woke up, he noticed gusts of snow blowing past the mouth of his cave. That was natural enough. What was unnatural was that the snow was blue.

"Why, that's beautiful!" Paul said. And he pulled on his red-and-black mackinaw coat, his corn-yellow scarf, and his snow boots. Then grinning from ear to ear, he set out across the blue hills.

The snow fell until the woods were covered with a thick blanket of blue. As Paul walked over huge drifts, bitter winds whistled through the trees and thunder rolled in the sky. But he soon began to hear another sound in the wind—"Maa-maa."

"Who's there?" Paul called.

"Maa-maa."

"Who's there?" said Paul again. His heart was starting to break, for the cries sounded as if they were coming from a baby crying for its mother and father.

"Maa-maa."

"Where are you, baby?" Suddenly Paul saw a tail sticking right up out of a blue snowdrift. When he pulled on the tail, out came the biggest baby ox on earth. Except for its white horns, the creature was frozen deep blue, the same color as the snow.

"He-ey, babe!" Paul shouted.

"Maa-maa-maa."

"Hush, hush, hush, babe," Paul whispered as he carried the frozen ox back home.

"There now," he said, setting the blue creature gently down in front of his fire. "We'll get you warmed up all right."

Paul fell asleep with his arm around the giant baby ox. He didn't know if the frozen babe would live or not. But when the morning sun began shining on the blue snow outside the cave, Paul felt a soft, wet nose nuzzling his neck. As the rough tongue licked his cheeks and nose and eyelids, Paul's joyous laughter shook the earth. He had found a friend.

Paul Bunyan and Babe the Blue Ox were inseparable after that. Babe grew so fast that Paul liked to close his eyes for a minute, count to ten, then look to see how much Babe had grown. Sometimes the ox would be a whole foot taller. It's a known fact that Babe's full-grown height was finally measured to be forty-two ax handles, and he weighed more than the combined weight of all the fish that ever got away. Babe was so big that when he and Paul trekked through the forests, Paul had to look through a telescope just to see what Babe's hind legs were doing.

In those times, huge sections of America were filled with dark green forests. And the forests were filled with trees—oceans of trees—trees as far as the eye could see—trees so tall you had to look straight up to see if it was morning, and maybe if you were lucky, you'd catch a glimpse of blue sky.

It would be nice if those trees could have stayed tall and thick forever. But the pioneers needed them to build houses, churches, ships, wagons, bridges, and barns. So one day Paul Bunyan took a good look at all those trees and said, "Babe, stand back. I'm about to invent logging.

"Tim-ber!" he yelled, and he swung his bright steel ax in a

wide circle. There was a terrible crash, and when Paul looked around, he saw he'd felled ten white pines with a single swing.

Paul bundled up the trees and loaded them onto the ox's back. "All right, Babe," he said. "Let's haul 'em to the Big Onion and send 'em down to a sawmill."

Since both Babe and Paul could cover a whole mile in a single step, it took them only about a week to travel from Maine to the Big Onion River in Minnesota.

"She's too crooked. Our logs will get jammed at her curves," Paul said to Babe as he peered through his telescope at the long, winding river. "Let's see what we can do about that." He tied one end of the rope to Babe's harness and the other around the end of the river. Then he shouted, "Pull! Pull!"

And Babe huffed and puffed until he pulled all the kinks out of that winding water.

"There! She's as straight as a gun barrel now," Paul said. "Let's send down these logs."

After that Paul and Babe traveled plenty fast through the untamed North Woods. They cut pine, spruce, and red willow in Minnesota, Michigan, and Wisconsin. They cleared cottonwoods out of Kansas so farmers could plant wheat. They cleared oaks out of Iowa so farmers could plant corn. It seems that the summer after the corn was planted in Iowa, there was a heat wave. It got so hot the corn started to pop. It popped until the whole state was covered with ten feet of popcorn. The wind blew the popcorn over to Kansas, where it fell like a blizzard. Unfortunately, the Kansas cows thought it *was* a blizzard and immediately froze to death.

When next heard of, Paul and Babe were headed to Arizona. Paul dragged his pickax behind him on that trip, not realizing he was leaving a big ditch in his tracks. Today that ditch is called the Grand Canyon.

When they got back from out west, Paul and Babe settled down on the Big Onion River. One night, after the two had spent the day rolling thousands of logs down the river, Paul was so tired he couldn't even see straight. As he lay under the stars, his giant body aching, he said, "Babe, it's time I started me a logging camp. I'm gonna hire a bunch of fellers to help me."

You might say this was a turning point for Paul Bunyan. Not for thirty years, since the day his parents had left him crying all alone in that Maine cave, had he asked a single human being for help. But the next day Paul and Babe hiked all over the northern timberlands, posting signs that said:

LOGGERS NEEDED TO WORK FOR PAUL BUNYAN.
IF INTERESTED,
COME TO BIG ONION, MINNESOTA, TO APPLY.

Word spread fast. Since all the woodsmen had heard of Paul Bunyan, hundreds of thousands of them hurried to Big Onion, eager to be part of his crew.

Paul wanted the biggest and brawniest men for his camp, so he made an announcement to all the men who'd gathered to apply for the job. "There's only two requirements," he said. "All my loggers have to be over ten feet tall and able to pop six buttons off their shirts with one breath."

Well, about a thousand of the lumberjacks met those requirements, and Paul hired them all. Then he built a gigantic logging camp with bunkhouses a mile long and bunks ten beds high. The camp's chow table was so long that it took a week to pass the salt and pepper from one end to the other. Paul and Babe dug a few ponds to provide drinking water for everyone. Today we call those ponds the Great Lakes.

But feeding that crew of giants was a bigger problem. One day

Paul's cook, Sourdough Sam, said to Paul, "Boss, there's no way I can make enough flapjacks for these hungry fellers. Every morning the ones who don't get seconds threaten to kill me."

The next day Paul built Sam a flapjack griddle the size of an ice-skating rink. Then he lit a forest fire underneath that burned night and day.

"But how'm I supposed to grease this thing?" Sam asked.

"Every morning before dawn we'll get a hundred men to strap bacon fat to the bottoms of their shoes and skate around the griddle till you're ready to cook," Paul said.

Well, after Paul got the flapjack griddle all squared away, he figured he needed a bookkeeper to keep track of all the food bills. So he hired a man named Johnny Inkslinger. Johnny kept the payroll, and he took care of Babe's hay and grain bills, and about ten thousand and two other things. He used a fountain pen that was twenty feet long and connected by a giant hose to a lake filled with ink. It's said that Johnny figured out he could save over four hundred and twenty gallons of ink a year just by not crossing his *t*'s and dotting his *i*'s.

Everything at the Big Onion Lumber Company ran pretty smoothly until the year of the Hard Winter. That winter it was so cold that one day Shot Gunderson, Paul's foreman, rode up to Paul's shanty on his saddled bear with a whole list of problems.

"Boss, we've got trouble!" he said. "When the fellers go out to work, their feet are getting so frostbitten, they're starting to fall off."

"That's bad," Paul said, scratching his beard. "Well, tell the fellers to let their whiskers grow. Then when their beards get down to their feet, they can knit them into socks."

"Good thinkin'," said Shot.

"What else?" said Paul.

"The flames for all the lanterns are freezing!"

"Well, just take the frozen flames outside and store them somewhere," Paul said. "Then wait for them to melt in the spring."

"Great idea," said Shot.

"What else?" said Paul.

"Just one more thing—when I give orders to the woods crew, all my words freeze in the air and hang there stiff as icicles."

"Oh, well, get Babe to haul your frozen words away and store them next to the lantern flames. They'll thaw out in the spring too," Paul said.

Sure enough, the beard socks kept the men's feet from freezing and falling off, and the lantern flames and Shot's words all thawed out in the spring. The only problem was that when the lantern flames melted, they caused some mean little brushfires. And when Shot's frozen words thawed, old cries of *"Timber!"* and *"Chow time!"* started to echo throughout the woods, causing all sorts of confusion. But other than that, things ran pretty smoothly at the Big Onion Lumber Company until the spring of the China Rains.

One day that spring, Shot Gunderson burst into Paul's shanty with his pant legs soaking wet. "Boss, we've got a problem! The rains are starting to come *up* from the ground instead of *down* from the sky."

"They must be coming from China," said Paul. "Order two thousand umbrellas. When they come, cut the handles off and replace them with snowshoe straps."

Shot did as Paul said, and soon all the loggers were wearing umbrellas on their shoes to keep the China Rains from shooting up their pant legs.

Unfortunately, the China Rains caused a crop of ten-foot mosquitoes to attack the camp. The men tried using chicken wire for mosquito nets. Then they started barricading the doors and windows of the bunkhouse with two-ton boulders to keep them out. Finally they had to vacate the bunkhouse altogether when the mosquitoes tore off the roof.

"Get some giant bumblebees," Paul ordered Shot. "They'll get rid of the mosquitoes."

Shot did as Paul said. The only problem was, the bees and the mosquitoes fell madly in love, and soon they were having children. Since the children had stingers on both ends, they caught the loggers both coming and going!

But Paul finally outsmarted the bee-squitoes.

"If there's one thing a bee-squito loves more than stinging, it's sweets," Paul said. So he got them to swarm to a Hawaiian sugar ship docked in Lake Superior. And when the whole bunch got too fat to move, he shipped them to a circus in Florida.

Well, there's stories and stories about Paul Bunyan, Babe the Blue Ox, and the Big Onion Lumber Company. For many years old loggers sat around potbellied stoves and told about the good old times with Paul. They told how Paul and Babe logged all the trees in Minnesota, then moved on to Washington, Oregon, and Alaska. And when last heard of, the two were somewhere off the Arctic Circle.

The old loggers are all gone now, but many of their stories still hang frozen in the cold forest air of the North Woods, waiting to be told. Come spring, when they start to thaw, some of them might just start telling themselves. It's been known to happen.

BIBLIOGRAPHY

The following list includes my primary sources, along with the many other books and articles that were helpful to me in these retellings.

DAVY CROCKETT

Blair, Walter. *Tall Tale America.* Coward-McCann Inc., Publishers, 1944.

Clough, Ben C. *The American Imagination at Work.* Alfred A. Knopf, Inc., 1947.

Coffin, Tristram Potter, and Cohen, Hennig, eds. *The Parade of Heroes: Legendary Figures in American Lore.* Anchor Press/Doubleday & Co., 1978.

Dorson, Richard M. *America in Legend: Folklore from the Colonial Period to the Present.* Pantheon Books, 1973.

Dorson, Richard M., ed. *Davy Crockett: American Comic Legend.* Rockland Editions, 1939.

Flanagan, John T., and Hudson, Arthur Palmer. *The American Folklore Era.* A. S. Barnes & Co., 1958.

Lofaro, Michael, ed. *The Tall Tales of Davy Crockett, 1839–1841.* University of Tennessee Press, 1987.

Malcolmson, Anne. *Yankee Doodle's Cousins.* Houghton Mifflin Co., 1941.

Rourke, Constance. *Davy Crockett.* Harcourt, Brace & Company, 1934.

Sketches and Eccentricities of Colonel David Crockett of West Tennessee. J. and J. Harper, 1833.

BIBLIOGRAPHY

SALLY ANN THUNDER ANN WHIRLWIND

Dorson, Richard M., ed. *Davy Crockett: American Comic Legend*. Rockland Editions, 1939.

Lofaro, Michael, ed. *The Tall Tales of Davy Crockett, 1839–1841*. University of Tennessee Press, 1987.

JOHNNY APPLESEED

Blair, Walter. *Tall Tale America*. Coward-McCann Inc., Publishers, 1944.

Botkin, Benjamin A., ed. *A Treasury of American Folklore*. Crown Publishers, 1944.

Clough, Ben C. *The American Imagination at Work*. Alfred A. Knopf, Inc., 1947.

Coffin, Tristram Potter, and Cohen, Hennig. *Folklore: From the Working Folk of America*. Anchor Press/Doubleday & Co., 1973.

Hatcher, Harlan. *The Buckeye Country*. G. P. Putnam & Sons, 1940.

Malcolmson, Anne. *Yankee Doodle's Cousins*. Houghton Mifflin Co., 1941.

Price, Robert. "Johnny Appleseed: Man and Myth." In *The Life Treasury of American Folklore*. Time Inc., 1961.

Sandburg, Carl. *Abraham Lincoln*. Harcourt, Brace & Company, 1926.

Wecter, Dixon. *The Hero in America: A Chronicle of Hero-Worship*. Charles Scribner's Sons, 1942.

STORMALONG

Blair, Walter. *Tall Tale America*. Coward-McCann Inc., Publishers, 1944.

Brown, Charles Edward. *Old Stormalong Yarns*. C. E. Brown, 1933.

Carmer, Carl. *The Hurricane's Children*. Farrar & Rinehart, Inc., 1937.

Malcolmson, Anne. *Yankee Doodle's Cousins*. Houghton Mifflin Co., 1941.

Shay, Frank, ed. *American Sea Songs & Chanteys*. Arno Press, 1948.

Shay, Frank. *Here's Audacity! American Legendary Heroes*. Arno Press, 1930.

Stoutenburg, Adrien. *American Tall Tales*. Viking Press, 1966.

MOSE

Asbury, Herbert. *The Gangs of New York*. Garden City Pub., 1927.

Asbury, Herbert. *Ye Olde Fire Laddies*. Alfred A. Knopf, Inc., 1930.

BIBLIOGRAPHY

Blair, Walter. *Tall Tale America*. Coward-McCann Inc., Publishers, 1944.

Butler, Benjamin. *A Glance at New York*. Samuel French, 1848.

Dayton, Abram C. *Last Days of Knickerbocker Life*. George W. Harlan, 1882.

Dorson, Richard M. *America in Legend: Folklore from the Colonial Period to the Present*. Pantheon Books, 1973.

Harlow, Alvin F. *Old Bowery Days*. D. Appleton & Co., 1931.

Jagendorf, M. *Upstate Downstate*. Vanguard Press, Inc., 1949.

Kernan, Frank. *Reminiscences of the Old Fire Laddies*. New York, 1885.

New York City Fire Museum.

FEBOLD FEBOLDSON

Beath, Paul R. "Febold Feboldson: Tall Tales from the Great Plains." In *The Life Treasury of American Folklore*. Time Inc., 1961.

Blair, Walter. *Tall Tale America*. Coward-McCann Inc., Publishers, 1944.

Botkin, Benjamin A., ed. *A Treasury of American Folklore*. Crown Publishers, 1944.

Coffin, Tristram Potter, and Cohen, Hennig, eds. *The Parade of Heroes: Legendary Figures in American Lore*. Anchor Press/Doubleday & Co., 1978.

Malcolmson, Anne. *Yankee Doodle's Cousins*. Houghton Mifflin Co., 1941.

Southern Folklore Quarterly (September 1943).

PECOS BILL

Boatright, Mody C. "Tall Tales from Texas." In *The Life Treasury of American Folklore*. Time Inc., 1961.

Botkin, Benjamin A., ed. *A Treasury of American Folklore*. Crown Publishers, 1944.

Bowman, James Cloyd. *Pecos Bill*. Albert Whitman, & Co., 1938.

Coffin, Tristram Potter, and Cohen, Hennig, eds. *The Parade of Heroes: Legendary Figures in American Lore*. Anchor Press/Doubleday & Co., 1978.

Felton, Harold. *Pecos Bill, Texas Cowpuncher*. Alfred A. Knopf, Inc., 1949.

Journal of American Folklore. (January–June 1941).

Malcolmson, Anne. *Yankee Doodle's Cousins*. Houghton Mifflin Co., 1941.

Shay, Frank. *Here's Audacity! American Legendary Heroes*. Arno Press, 1930.

BIBLIOGRAPHY

JOHN HENRY

Blair, Walter. *Tall Tale America*. Coward-McCann Inc., Publishers, 1944.

Carmer, Carl. *The Hurricane's Children*. Farrar & Rinehart, Inc., 1937.

Chappell, Louis W. *John Henry: A Folk-Lore Study*. Walter Biedermann, 1933.

Johnson, Guy. *John Henry*. University of North Carolina Press, 1929.

Malcolmson, Anne. *Yankee Doodle's Cousins*. Houghton Mifflin Co., 1941.

Roark, Bradford. *John Henry*. Arno Press, 1931.

Shay, Frank. *Here's Audacity! American Legendary Heroes*. Arno Press, 1930.

Stoutenburg, Adrien. *American Tall Tales*. Viking Press, 1966.

PAUL BUNYAN

Blair, Walter. *Tall Tale America*. Coward-McCann Inc., Publishers, 1944.

Bowman, James Cloyd. *The Adventures of Paul Bunyan*. Century Co., 1927.

Carmer, Carl. *The Hurricane's Children*. Farrar & Rinehart, Inc., 1937.

Laughead, W. B. *Paul Bunyan*. Red River Lumber Co., 1916.

Malcolmson, Anne. *Yankee Doodle's Cousins*. Houghton Mifflin Co., 1941.

McCormick, Dell J. *Paul Bunyan Swings His Ax*. Caxton Printers, Ltd., 1936.

Rounds, Glen. *Ol' Paul, the Mighty Logger*. Holiday House, Inc., 1949.

Shay, Frank. *Here's Audacity! American Legendary Heroes*. Arno Press, 1930.

Shephard, Esther. *Paul Bunyan*. Harcourt, Brace & World, Inc., 1952.

Stevens, James. *Paul Bunyan*. Alfred A. Knopf, Inc., 1925.

Stevens, James. *The Saginaw Paul Bunyan*. Alfred A. Knopf, Inc., 1932.

Turney, Ida Virginia. *Paul Bunyan Comes West*. Houghton Mifflin Co., 1928.

◆ ◆ ◆

The following is a list of sources that were helpful in writing the introductions to the tall tales.

Boorstin, Daniel J. *The Americans: The National Experience*. Vintage Books, 1965.

Brown, Carolyn S. *The Tall Tale*. University of Tennessee Press, 1987.

Dick, Everett. *Conquering the Great American Desert*. Nebraska State Historical Society, 1975.

Gosnell, Harper Allen. *Before the Mast in the Clippers.* Derrydale Press, 1937.

Hoffman, Daniel G. *Paul Bunyan: Last of the Frontier Demigods.* University of Pennsylvania Press, 1952.

Lynn, Kenneth S. *Mark Twain & Southwestern Humor.* Greenwood Press, Inc., 1960.

Nimrod, J. L. *Johnny Appleseed.* Chicago Historical Society, 1926. In Wecter, Dixon. *The Hero in America: A Chronicle of Hero-Worship.* Charles Scribner's Sons, 1942.

Prospector, Cowhand, and Sodbuster. United States Department of Interior, 1967.

Rourke, Constance. *American Humor.* Harcourt, Brace & Company, 1931.

MARY POPE OSBORNE's marvelous retellings of legends for children include *Favorite Greek Myths* and *Beauty and the Beast*, which *Newsweek* hailed as "destined to become a household classic." Versatile and prolific, she is the author of highly acclaimed picture books (most recently *Moonhorse*), middle-grade biographies of Benjamin Franklin and George Washington, and novels for young adults. She and her husband, Will, divide their time between New York City and Pennsylvania.

MICHAEL McCURDY has designed and illustrated many books, including *The Owl-Scatterer,* a *New York Times* Best Illustrated Children's Book of 1986. He has also written books for young readers, including *Hannah's Farm: Seasons on an Early American Homestead.* Mr. McCurdy lives with his wife, Deborah, and their two children on an old farm in the Berkshire Hills of Massachusetts.